CELEBRISI'S
JOURNEY

CELEBRISI'S JOURNEY

A NOVEL BY DAVID ROUNDS

TEN THOUSAND BUDDHAS PRESS
THE BUDDHIST TEXT TRANSLATION SOCIETY
SAN FRANCISCO   1976

Published by The Buddhist Text Translation Society, an affiliate of the Sino-American Buddhist Association, Gold Mountain Monastery, 1731 Fifteenth Street, San Francisco, CA 94103.

Distributed by Book People, 2940 Seventh Street, Berkeley, CA 94710 and The Book Bin, 547 Howard Street, San Francisco, CA 94105.

Cover drawing and design by Jim Gorman.

This work is fictional in its entirety, and any resemblance in it to persons living or dead or to institutions past or existing is purely coincidental, except in the case of the Millinocket mills, where the resemblance is entirely superficial.

The method of slaughtering pigs described in Chapter VI of this work was outlawed in part by an Act of Congress, in 1958. Livestock must now be rendered unconscious by gunshot, carbon dioxide gas, or mechanical or electrical stunning before it is shackled and hung for slaughter.

ISBN 0-917512-14-6
Library of Congress Catalog Card No. 76-28912

ACKNOWLEDGEMENTS

The author wishes to record his heartfelt gratitude to his teacher, the Venerable Master Hsuan Hua, Abbot of Gold Mountain Monastery, for the Master's unfailing compassionate guidance through the author's many failings; and also to record his gratitude to Bhiksu Heng Kuan and all the monks and nuns of Gold Mountain, for their teaching and friendship; to his wife Susan Rounds, for her loyalty, patience, intelligence, and help in the face of many obstacles; and to his parents, Stowell and Carol Rounds, his elder brother Tom Rounds, and his younger brother John Rounds, for their loyalty and constant kindnessess;

Also, to Kim Lee, of K & M Instant Typesetting Service in San Francisco, who had the manuscript typeset without remuneration to himself, as a donation to the publisher; to Jim Gorman, who took time from his own work to do the cover-illustration; to Louis Asekoff, for his ever-timely good words; and to Ronald B. Epstein and the many other friends who by encouragement, interest, and advice have supported the author in this work.

If there is any merit in this novel, the author dedicates it to the benefit of all beings, in the hope that anger and hatred will be lessened in the world.

"When you die and have been cremated to ashes, where have you gone? To find the 'you' of your true nature, which does not die, is the spiritual exercise of Ch'an. When your meditation reaches the point that the mountains are leveled, the seas disappear, and you doubt that there's a way at all, then suddenly, there beyond the dark willow and the bright flowers is another village. Although you felt there was no way, there is yet another world, another realm — the realm of light peace. Those who can bring their meditation to the ultimate point can experience freedom, independence, and the bliss of both body and mind — a bliss which is incomparable."

Ch'an Master Hsuan Hua

ONE

I WAS THE kind of person who never completely grows up after leaving high school. No one would have been able to tell it on the surface. I went into the service like everybody else, and I got married like everybody else. I lived with my wife Margherita and our little kid Vincent, Vin for short, in a two-family house off Bergenline Avenue, in West New York, New Jersey, which is where I'm from. Joseph R. Celebrisi, Joey to my friends, five years running I went on the night-shift to operate a hilo, what they call a fork-lift truck, in a truck-freight terminal in Ridgefield Park. I was fairly content with my life. When I say I hadn't grown up, I don't mean that I hung out on the street or threw away the rent-money on cards. I had clean habits; I took care of my family. But I couldn't give up the stunts.

We did the stunts in order to stand something solemn on its head. We'd done them since high-school: myself, and Jimmy DiLorenzo, who'd been my best friend since kindergarten, and Steve Zabrancewski from Jersey City, who Jimmy had met in the high-school baseball circuit. At first the stunts were nothing but practical jokes, but later they became very intense and elaborate. Once we wired the Jersey City Armory so that all the lights went out during Army National Guard exercises. Another time, we dressed up as policemen and kidnapped a crook named Herbie the Walnut, who was boss of the Jersey City mob, and we sent him up in a hot-air balloon over Newark Bay. He came down after a while and was rescued by a Japanese freighter carrying Toyotas. Margherita, my wife, was convinced that the mob would track us down and pack us in concrete and toss us off the end of a garbage-barge. But I figured we'd never get caught at the stunts. How could anybody trace us? It was impossible. The whole point of the stunts, the way I'd come to see it, was to forget who I was and become someone else. Instead of my usual respectable working-person self who would never do anything crazy to jeopardize his family, here I'd be concentrating everything on closing an Armory circuit before the night-patrol was due, or coming on to a mobster like I was the police, pouring myself up to the hilt into acting like somebody I wasn't; then who was I, at that moment? "Who's Celebrisi?" I'd ask myself. For a few minutes, I wouldn't completely know. And then for hours afterward, I'd have a tremendous feeling of happiness and energy.

Back then, I couldn't have said why I wanted this feeling of being changed into somebody else. It never crossed my mind to ask myself about it. It wasn't that I didn't think about things, but what I thought about was cars, having laughs, other people's faults, and humming through life without running into obstacles. There was nothing to force me to question things, until the monsignor stunt broke my life open.

The monsignor stunt was Jimmy's idea. "Maybe the new monsignor isn't normal," he said; I remember we were discussing it in the garage where Jimmy worked, on Kennedy Boulevard. He was taking a muffler off a 1957 Nash, which was the last year they made them. The new monsignor hadn't been in the parish a month and had already irritated practically everybody. He was young and tall and a bit soft in the face, with dark hair he wore in waves a bit too long, and he blinked when he looked down on you, and people said he talked like a book, which is not a compliment in the kind of neighborhood that I grew up in. People felt he probably spent a lot of time up in his apartments taking baths with a lot of scrubbing, so as to get the smell of decent working people off of him. The straw that broke the camel's back was the Fleetwood limousine. The priest who had preceded him, the old Irish monsignor, who had just retired, had used to make parish calls in a dove-grey Fleetwood Cadillac; I remember you could just catch a glimpse of his black hat-brim in the oval back-window. Now that the old priest had left, people naturally assumed that whatever new priest the archdiocese sent would have the decency to sell the limousine. No. The new monsignor fired the chauffeur and drove the thing himself. People became very indignant. Someone started the rumor that the monsignor was abnormal in matters of sex, and immediately everyone believed it. It allowed them to write him off.

"Maybe he is a deviant, and maybe he isn't; how are you going to prove it?" is what Jimmy said.

"Follow him at night," Steve told him. "You couldn't lose that limousine."

"That isn't the point," Jimmy said. His idea was that it didn't matter what the poor priest's personal disposition actually was. Queer or not, straight, just shy maybe, crazy, whatever, if a person wants to look normal in these matters — and the look of things is all that people who gossip care about anyway — then he just has to have himself seen with a woman now and then, and the neighborhood starts talking about somebody else. But the new monsignor was in a very ruinous situation. He was a priest; how could he have himself seen with a woman? Even if he was breaking his vow of chastity, it would have to be done on the quiet. He was stuck. He couldn't repair his deviant reputation. The stunt was to repair it for him.

We went over to Manhattan to a used clothing loft where the theater actors go, and we dressed Steve up as a priest, since he was the only one tall enough to pass for the monsignor. Then Jimmy and I discovered that we'd each expected the other to dress up as the woman. We both refused to do it; it was beneath our idea of our dignity. To ask a real woman to join the stunt wouldn't have sat well with our wives, though, if they'd found out about it . So we were stumped for a while. But Jimmy was always a genius for coming up with the raw materials. He went back over to Manhattan and found an actual deviant whose disposition was to dress as a woman by choice. This is the kind of confusion I was involved in.

It was June, eleven years ago. The person Jimmy had found, whose name was Cinderella, said she'd play the woman in the monsignor stunt for three-fifty an hour. We had to refer to her as "her"; nobody could have told she wasn't a woman. She told us that until a year before, she had been married to a woman and had had a job working a road-grader for the Town of Kearny Public Works Department. It made my mind reel. I couldn't get it out of my head that somebody could have changed so much. She was very sweet-tempered, too; she liked department stores and clothes and mah-jhong; she was happy. It made my little games of changing into somebody else on the stunts look like nothing. I kept wanting to ask her how she'd done it and what it felt like to actually become another person. But I never got around to it. I didn't want to embarrass her.

Cinderella made herself up as a forty-five-year-old divorcee from North Bergen. Grey lines down by the mouth, we hardly recognized her, and she blackened Steve's eyebrows and built up his nose and chin with some kind of putty, so that in a dim light we couldn't tell him from the new monsignor. Steve said it was really a stunt on him. Every Thursday night for a month, the two of them made the rounds of the night-spots in Jersey City. Jimmy hung around the edges to keep an eye on Steve and watch for

4

police. Pretty soon everybody's mother was saying the new monsignor must be all right: it was rumored he had been definitely seen with a woman. It had worked. We'd planned to stop right there. But the trouble was that here was a stunt, and Jimmy and I had had just about nothing to do with it. We were envious for action.

We began inventing decorations. Jimmy and I dressed up as seminarians, and the four of us rented a rowboat and went fishing in the Hudson River off the Weehawken piers. I caught a catfish with a face like a demon out of hell. The next day we decided to row across the river to Manhattan. Steve said we were crazy, but Jimmy and I could always talk faster than he could. Halfway across the river, we were spotted by the WCBS traffic-helicopter on duty over the West Side Highway. The reporter flew over us, and we heard ourselves described over Cinderella's pocket-radio. The reporter kept referring to us and joking about us with his anchorman. We docked alongside a luxury ocean-liner at the Forty-Second-Street pier, which was packed with shouting tourists and baggage and taxicabs. The radio news-show had sent out a reporter to ask us what priests might be doing crossing the Hudson in a rowboat. Someone tried to take a picture of us. With our hats in our faces, the front page of the *Jersey Journal* had us right up top in the morning.

Was this really the new monsignor from West New York? People weren't sure any more. They argued in the diners and the bars about whether the priest in the photo in the *Journal* was too heavy-set to be the monsignor, or maybe it was him and he just looked heavy-set because of the camera-angle? We were a success. The monsignor was a success. The whole parish flocked to St. Mary of the Fields' to hear this mystery-man say Mass and give his sermons, which were full of little jokes and educated quotations and exhortations to be thoughtful of our fellow man.

Steve resigned. He said he wasn't doing another stunt for a good long while, if ever. But the rest of us couldn't resist another

5

decoration. Two nights later, the three of us stole the new monsignor's Fleetwood limousine from its parking-place in front of the parish residence. We put the car on the lift in Jimmy's garage, made cut-outs in the muffler, and jacked up the rear suspension: the kind of thing you see in high-school parking-lots. We put powder on my hair and dressed me up as the old chauffeur, set Cinderella in the back seat, with Jimmy in priest's clothes propped up on cushions beside her, and we roared down Bergenline Avenue at nine-thirty in the morning.

Bergenline is the main street of West New York, full of gift-shops and beauty-salons, bargain stores and groceries and pizza parlors and newsstands where bets are placed, and at nine-thirty in the morning there are a lot of people there. Our plan was to drive five blocks, turn off, ditch the limousine, and disappear. It didn't happen. Our audience turned our heads. People poured out of the stores; kids ran up and pounded on the windows; the town was wound up like a top for the monsignor's next act, and here it was. When I'd driven the five blocks we'd planned, I didn't even ask the others; I just swung the limousine around and drove back down the avenue again. We went up and down Bergenline nine times. The cut-outs made a racket they must have heard in Secaucus on the far side of the Jersey Swamp. Jimmy gave benedictions in the oval back window. I had it up to nearly sixty and did the cleanest racing-changes of my life. Who was going to flag down a monsignor? The cops just stared. I believe we could have got clean away even then. But none of us knew what we were doing or who we were any more. I drove that Fleetwood all around West New York; I probably would have tried to drive it across the bottom of the Hudson River and up the sides of the Empire State Building if anyone had asked me. To us, this was the finest stunt of all.

Someone finally went and jimmied the police commissioner out from behind his desk, and when we went down Jackson Street, which is narrow, there was the commissioner parked broadside to our path in his personal car. He took his cap off his head and walked up reverentially to the new monsignor, until he saw it wasn't the new monsignor at all but Jimmy DiLorenzo, the night-mechanic at the Shell station on Kennedy Boulevard. He went instantly red, and shouting burst out of him.

I didn't hear a word he said. Getting out of that car, looking around, I was absorbed in that stunt-feeling of being somebody else, only it seemed a hundred times stronger than before, as if the feeling had been supercharged along with the limousine. It seemed to me then that the place in my brain where I ordinarily had my thoughts had been jacked up an inch out of my head, as if there was a hole now in the top of my skull, and my mind was open to the sky. There was a window in my mind, and some kind of invisible energy was pouring out from it and mingling with the outside air. I wondered if my forgetting who I was in the stunt had lifted some kind of lid off me. The energy seemed to be spreading out into the street and flowing over the cars. As it touched things, they changed. They seemed light and distant and slowed down; they could have been under a charm. I thought everything around me was pushed a few feet away, like behind a glass in a diorama, and an animated show was going on in there, with people milling around and the police commissioner puffing and waving his arms, all seeming to be mechanized, like those little figurines that come jerking out the front of cuckoo-clocks when the hour strikes noon. That first day, I don't believe I had any thought that something might have gone wrong with my vision or my mind. Everything seemed too peaceful for anything wrong to have happened. Instead of feeling odd, I felt clean in my body, the way a person feels after swimming in a cool stream.

Suddenly the new monsignor himself was walking up beside his limousine. I hadn't noticed him before, but now he was staring at me very intently. I wondered if he could also see how everything was changed. As soon as I thought this, I believed it. I decided he was staring at me because he wanted to find out just who this other person was who knew how to let energy flow out of his mind. I told myself that what was happening must be showing somehow in my face. I felt very pleased with myself for figuring all this out. While I had these thoughts, the energy stopped flowing. In a moment, everything was normal again.

The monsignor was looking coolly around. Everybody including the police commissioner had shut up like a clam. The monsignor bent down for a look at the cut-outs and the jacked-up suspension on his limousine. Then he straightened up and said, "Commissioner Lacerra, I want you to know how very much I regret this incident. As you may have heard, the parish has been anxious to sell this limousine for quite a while, but we were unable to secure a buyer until Mr. DiLorenzo" — he meant Jimmy — "until Mr. DiLorenzo managed to locate a fancy automobile buff who wanted the car if it was modified in this manner. Mr. DiLorenzo out of Christian charity offered to do the work solely for the cost of the parts."

At first I thought maybe I'd missed something, but it was obvious that everybody there was thunderstruck at what the monsignor was saying. He pretended that he didn't notice. He had more to say in his sermon-giving voice about the temptation and distraction and source of discord that we all knew the limousine had been in the parish, not just to these young people (and he nodded toward us) but to everyone, clergy and layman alike — everyone murmured at that; he'd hit the right note — so he, the monsignor, would insist that the new owner drive the limousine only under proper and seemly conditions. He further would insist that he, the monsignor, be held wholly responsible for this regrettable incident, as he understood that no one was injured? and there was no damage to property?

He let it be known that he was finished. The commissioner didn't say anything. What could he have said? The monsignor opened a rear door of the limousine for Cinderella and ushered her inside, got in behind the wheel himself with Jimmy and me beside him, and he waited without a motion or a sound until the commissioner turned his car around and the crowd moved off the road. Then he started up the engine, said "Mary Mother of God" when he heard the blat of those cut-outs, and he drove us away. Still without saying anything, and with a small amused smile on his face as he drove, the monsignor sat politely through the noise of our thanking him and praising him for rescuing us. It was the first time I had seen him close at hand. He had the perfectly right features of the man in the magazine advertisement: square dimpled chin, straight nose, wavy dark hair, broad forehead. Only his eyes seemed like they might be a priest's, with a look in them half of good humor and half of thoughtfulness. I wondered if his handsome face embarrassed him. If he was vain about anything, I thought, it would have to be his bookish speech. When we had quieted down, he introduced himself — his name was Bolignioni — and then he asked us our names in turn, saying he'd been very curious to meet us. "I have something to thank you for," he said. "You let my parishioners know that I exist and also that we celebrate the Mass at their parish church, which they seemed to have forgotten. I presume it was you that put on those other performances as well?" — We admitted that it was. — "I must say you have a most peculiar way of propagating the faith," he said mildly. "Have you done it before?"

His treating it as something serious that aroused his curiosity made it look ridiculous. We were too embarrassed to say anything.

"Why did you do it?" he said.

Finally I answered, "There were some rumours going around, Father. We wanted to get rid of them. You know."

"No, I don't know," he said. "What were they?"

"I wouldn't want to say, Father. If people don't know something, then they invent it, that's all. We're real sorry if we embarrassed you."

"Did you embarrass me?" he said.

None of us would say.

"At any rate," he went on, with zest in his voice, "I wouldn't want to have missed that police commissioner: he was wonderful. It isn't every day you can have fun like that in these clothes I'm wearing. And this absurd limousine. Here I've been driving it for months because I thought it was expected of me. What's it worth, do you know? Do you think I could trade it in for a Peugeot?"

We stopped at Jimmy's garage, and while Jimmy and I put the limousine back to normal, the monsignor cross-examined us about cars, as if he was quite interested in them, and he asked us about our families. Our embarrassment wore off. He was our age, after all, and we could see that he wanted to be treated as just another person. I was itching to ask him about the stunt-feelings and the energy flowing out from my mind, but I didn't want to mention it with Jimmy there, since Jimmy would have nothing to do with the mental part of the stunts, and whenever I mentioned the subject, he would ride me about it. The monsignor dropped Cinderella off at her bus stop and took me home. As I was getting out of the car, he gave me a sharp look, the same look he had given me earlier in the street, when the energy had been pouring out. "It seems we have something to talk about, Joey," the monsignor said. "Come and see me."

"Okay, thank you, Father." I watched him drive off and thought to myself: What a stroke of luck! He did notice what was happening with me. Here's a friendly, educated guy, he's going to explain the whole thing to me. Do you suppose there's a way to make the energy pour out whenever you want it to?

That we were completely misinterpreting each other never occurred to me. It was natural for me to just assume that an educated priest might be able to explain mental happenings. I'd been raised a Catholic, the same as nearly everyone else in West New York. By the time I left parochial school after the third grade, I had a full store of the teaching-sisters' stories of miracles and visions and the rest. My father, who had no use for priests, instructed me very carefully that whatever they said in church was nothing but a lot of baloney — he made me promise not to tell my mother or my sister this, though. It was our secret among the males. But even a Catholic who has permanently lost his faith will believe that it's likely there are mysterious and visionary things. What he has decided is that whatever these things are, the Church has got them wrong. I just assumed that the stunt-feelings were something fairly ordinary as unusual things go, something intriguing, a source of amusement; that was all. You concentrate your mind on being someone else: don't children do the same when they dress up and pretend? When I was a kid, I often used to stare at things until my thoughts would seem to stop, and there would be a feeling of emptiness and light. Nothing bad had come of that; what could possibly be wrong with the stunt-feelings?

The truth is that I was already on the defensive about them. My wife Margherita had nothing but suspicion for the stunts and for anything associated with them. At first, before we were married, she took the stunts to just be crazy practical jokes — they weren't much more than that then — and she laughed along with the rest of us. My stunting fitted in with my habit of wisecracks and with a slightly irresponsible attitude I had, an edge of boredom with the regular routine, and that probably attracted her; her life had been very ordinary. Her parents weren't happy about me. They were Neapolitan in origin, like my family, and Margherita grew up in West New York the same as I did, but her people were better-class than mine were. My father is a clerk at the local post-office, while Margherita's father is a plumbing contractor with two employees, and his brother, Margherita's uncle, owns the fuel-oil-delivery business in town. Margherita had been popular in high school, and her people thought she could have done a lot better job of finding a husband afterwards. We laughed at them for it. Everybody our own age thought we were the perfect couple. But Margherita must have assumed all along that I would eventually change. I didn't change. She became more and more interested in the ordinary things of life, and I got even less interested than before. I kept making wisecracks and went on playing practical jokes, each one with more risk to it than the last. After Vin was born, she told me I'd have to cut the stunts out. She said it was too irresponsible with the baby now, considering that I could get caught and there'd be consequences. I told her sure, Margherita, okay. I didn't know then what happens when you get mixed up in a lie. We went ahead with the stunts on the sly.

So after the monsignor drove me home that day, I sailed upstairs to our part of the house full of vigor and excitement, and I burst through the front door and called out, "Hey, Margherita, did you hear what happened? Hey, I bet they got it on the news, did you have it on? Where's Vin, he's got to hear what his daddy's been doing."

Margherita didn't say a word to me; she didn't condescend to look at me. She is a small person, like myself, and when she was angry, her voice and body used to tremble like the emotion was too strong for her to hold it down; it would mortify her and she wouldn't speak. She just went into the kitchen where she'd been keeping the dinner hot — I was half an hour late — and she slapped down the plate in front of me like a waiter who thinks his restaurant is too high-class for your kind of person. I tried to soothe her down a little. "Look Margherita, I know you don't think too much of my doing another stunt, but I guess you heard I did, and it was really tremendous this time, absolutely no problems with the cops or anything, it went real smooth without a hitch, and listen, something very interesting happened; I mean very interesting."

Not a peep from her; not a word. She was shifting her food around on her plate with her fork and pushing her hair away from her forehead.

"You want to hear about it, Margherita?" I said. "Maybe you'd consider this is something you'd want to hear about?"

Nothing. After a minute or two — I'd become a little irritated — I told her the vegetables were cold; could she heat them up for me? She got up, took my plate, and scraped whatever it was into the garbage. I yelled at her for that, but she just sat down and stared at her plate again. Right then the coffee began boiling over on the stove. I reached over and grabbed her wrist and asked her could she hear? had she gone deaf? She looked up at me finally, with her dark eyes black, and she was shaking so that her head was almost nodding and the fork in her hand rang against her water-glass. She hissed at me that I should get my hands off her. I was amazed at this; I'd never heard her speak that way. "What's come over you?" I asked her. "What's come over you?"

I let go of her and turned the burner off. She was muttering, half to me, half not, which was her way of saying something without saying it: "He wants to know what's come over me. With him acting like a two-bit drifter, he wants to know this."

I told myself I was in too good a mood today to let her ruin it, so she was just going to have listen. "You're not understanding this," I told her. "It wasn't a two-bit anything. It was a perfectly all right thing we did. You could say we were trying to help the monsignor. He bailed us out from the cops, Margherita. He put the finishing touches on the stunt himself. He thanked us. There isn't going to be any charges brought, there isn't going to be any consequences. The most they can slap me with is reckless driving and maybe cop my license for thirty days, sixty days, and what's that? Eat your dinner. It's nothing." She looked like she was ready to throw her dinner at me. "Listen, Margherita, I wish you'd rest easy about this. I want you to know what happened in my mind. Everything changed while the stunt was going on. Everything around us suddenly looked beautiful and strange; I don't know if I can describe it. It was a hundred times better than the other stunts" —

She interrupted me, almost yelling at me: "That's right, because the other times you didn't have some slut along to get

13

your kicks with, you and your crummy friends."

That silenced me. It had never crossed my mind that she would think I'd been unfaithful to her: with Cinderella? It was ridiculous. But it was obviously what anyone might think.

"You had to do this in public," Margherita was saying, with her face tight and hardened, "and everybody knows about it, everybody sees just what you think of me."

"Listen, Margherita." I felt ashamed to tell her what the truth was.

"I'm not listening to you" —

"Yeah, but listen: this was a man. There wasn't any playing around, I never played around on the side ever, Margherita, I'm telling you. The person who played the woman in the monsignor stunt, she was a man."

Margherita didn't know what to say to this. It was even more mortifying than she had thought. She was looking at me as if she'd seen something slimy.

"I can see how it must have looked, Margherita," I was saying, "though actually, Cinderella is a very decent person, but I just didn't think of how people would see it. Maybe this is hard for you to believe, but I didn't? I just got all involved in the thing. I didn't mean to hurt you by it. We never meant to hurt anybody by the stunts. I just get all involved in what's happening in my mind, because sometimes it feels real beautiful, and then I don't think."

She was crying now. "You promised me, Joey. You made all these promises."

I'd gone around behind her place and put my arms around her shoulders. "I'm real sorry about this, Margherita. It was just a perfect opportunity. I didn't know it would hurt you."

"Have you done others, Joey? Without telling me, other of these things?"

"Yeah, I guess, one or two. I didn't think anything would happen. I see now. I won't do them any more." I meant it then, although I don't think she believed me.

"What's going to happen to you?" she was saying. "Carmella heard, she told me what you did this morning, you and Jimmy and Steve and that, and that person." Carmella is Margherita's sister: she lived with her husband and children downstairs from us.

"I don't want you to worry, Margherita. The monsignor's going to keep us in the clear. He said I should come see him, and he's going to explain what goes on in my mind, and there won't be any problem."

"He doesn't know anything, Joey. He's not anybody who can stop anything."

"Yes, he is. You calm down now; you calm down. He's going to clear up everything that happened."

It didn't turn out that way. Two days afterward, the archdiocese transferred the monsignor out of the parish. I went over to the parish-residence to find out where he'd been sent to, but nobody seemed to know. That same afternoon the police commissioner, the detective captain, a sergeant, and five patrolmen came roaring up to our house in four squad cars with sirens full blast, and they all trooped upstairs, and when he'd caught his breath the commissioner handed me a warrant for arrest on charges of breaking and entering and willful destruction of property. Somebody had broken into the parish garage and had spray-painted foul language all over the monsignor's limousine. Jimmy was already in custody in the back seat of one of the squad cars. They never found Cinderella, since it turned out none of us knew her address or her real name. Jimmy and I had both been at our jobs during the entire night that the garage had been broken into, so there was no basis for the charges against us. But they kept us in the city lock-up for fifteen days.

I'd never seen Margherita so depressed as she was during those visiting-hours. I kept telling her nothing would come of a false charge, because the union protects your job in a case like this, and I made promises and promises and promises that the stunts were finished whether we wanted it or not, because of the publicity. We sat there in the day-room arguing, while the old guard at his desk worked on a model sailing-ship. I tried to ignore him and to explain to Margherita the feeling of being someone else and the feeling of the energy pouring out from my mind, since I figured it would be easier on both of us if she'd understand, but she didn't understand, because I didn't understand. She didn't want to hear, she just wanted me to stop all this terrible crazy talk, she just wanted this to be over with, so we could go back to where we were. Okay, okay, I told her, but give me the benefit of the doubt, maybe there's nothing wrong in the mental part of the stunts, which is the only part I care about now anyway. Supposing I don't need the actual stunts for it? I can just do it at home. She didn't like hearing that. We had some angry words.

Then, for the last three or four days I was in the lock-up, she didn't come to visiting hours at all. That put the scare in me. When she hadn't come the second day, I got the guard to call home, but he said he couldn't get an answer. I figured maybe she'd moved back in with her parents, or she'd found another guy, she was petitioning for an annulment, she'd burnt the house down, all kinds of ideas went through my head. I tried to persuade the guard to call her parents or her sister Carmella, but no, he couldn't do it, he took a risk calling up my own house as it was.

They finally decided to hold what they called a preliminary hearing on the evidence; of course, there wasn't any evidence. Margherita wasn't in court; I was very upset by that. My mother and my sister Donna were in the audience, but the bailiff wouldn't give me permission to go ask them where my wife was and what had happened to her.

We had a lawyer named Bohanian. Margherita's uncle had got him for us: the uncle in the fuel-oil-delivery business. Bohanian saw his job as proclaiming some beautifully arranged sentences the point of which, as I noticed after a while, was to subtly insult his pals the judge and the police and the assistant district attorney and the marshall and the ancient reporter from the *Hud-*

son Dispatch. They were all winking and chuckling and smiling there together and busily creating a mysterious atmosphere for the defendants and the audience. The hearing took hours, with recesses and a lunch break and different cases going on all at once and the judge, whose name was Schlemmer, ordering the windows closed then opened then closed, and everybody up front at the bench there snickering with each other. Schlemmer finally did us the favor of ruling that there were no grounds for the charges, and then he delivered us a lecture on proper respect for the law and told us the fifteen days we'd spent in jail were far too few as far as he was concerned. Bohanian told us that he'd tried to keep the costs down, but that he'd have to charge us two hundred and fifty dollars. I thought that I'd be able to ask my sister what had happened to Margherita, but they didn't let me talk to her until they'd kept us waiting for an hour and a half in the clerk's office.

Margherita had taken a job. For some reason, of all the things I thought she might be doing while I was in jail, this obvious thing had never occurred to me. It seemed like the worst thing she could have done to me. It wasn't that a lot of women we knew didn't go to a job; Margherita had worked herself, before Vin was born. But she hadn't consulted me this time, she hadn't even told me: she'd just left me in jail like she'd given me up for worthless, like she couldn't trust me to bring home a pay-check any more. I was just some kind of nuisance factor now. Without any certain idea of what I was going to do, but with a thousand agitated thoughts streaming through my mind, I drove over to Bergenline Avenue to a beauty-salon named Lyle's, where my sister had said Margherita was working. I parked in front of the place and barged in. It was crowded with Greek statuettes and tall vases of permanent flowers and a fountain and large lamps with drooping shades made of colored cut glass. At the end of two rows of women reading magazines in white ironwork chairs, I found Margherita at the receptionist's desk, almost hidden by a tropical fish-tank. I told her for God's sake, before something happens, would she come on home.

It was the same as before: she didn't say anything at all. She shook her head a half-inch and looked down at her appointment book, as if I was a man she didn't know who was trying to bother her on the bus. I asked her would she please? Would she listen to what I said? I was shouting at her under my breath, and I could feel the women in the ironwork chairs prick up their ears and begin staring at us over their magazines. I took hold of Margherita by the arm and yelled in a whisper: "You're coming home with me where you belong, you do as I tell you."

She had her fists doubled up on either side of the blotter on her desk, and she wouldn't look at me. All she said was: "Get home."

I began yelling at her out loud. "What is this, the house isn't good enough for you any more? Me and Vin, we aren't good enough for you? I'm so on the skids I can't make the payments now, I can't even earn enough to keep you in dresses, is that it? You ever thought of making your own dresses, like plenty of decent women do? I didn't miss a paycheck in five years before this crazy thing, which wasn't my fault, but because you want fancy clothes, it has to get around that I can't keep you provided for." I'd somehow convinced myself that the whole problem had to do with her clothes, and I blabbered on at her how I could get a Saturday job if she felt she had to have a new wardrobe, and how this or that shop had been advertising a sale — I don't know what else. In a minute her boss, Lyle the hairdresser, a pint-sized man around forty-five with a moustache and gold-rimmed glasses and perfectly clean fingernails, rushed in from out back, gripped my arm with a numbing-tight hold, and walked me down through the statuettes and staring women and plastic flowers and shoved me stumbling out onto the sidewalk. Right away I was back at the door, yanking and banging, but he'd locked it, and I yelled at the top of my lungs, "You come home, you're coming home or you'll regret this, Margherita"—

I remember getting into my car and pulling away from the curb into the avenue; then my mind blanked out for about four hours. From the rest of the afternoon and on into the evening only two pictures were still in my memory afterwards: one of me sitting on the edge of our bed in our bedroom, and the other of me cleaning up some pieces of metal on the bedroom floor. Margherita had an adjustable wire dress-form which her mother had given her, but which she'd never used; she kept it in the back of the bedroom closet. What I'd done while my mind was blanked out — as we figured it out later — was to come home, pull out the dress-form, smash it to bits, and then sweep it up into a neat pile in the middle of the floor. Then I drove to my job at the truck terminal, punched in, explained to the shop-steward that the charges against me had been dropped, started up my hilo, and went to work; and I might have been asleep the whole time, for all I knew of what was happening.

The pieces of freight that take the most skill to handle with the hilo are long heavy pipes and drive-shafts; they tend to roll off the hilo-prongs, especially around the turns. You run into them three or four times a week. That night, I had to take some steel pipe off a straight-job — what they call a short truck without a trailer; and suddenly I heard a voice saying very close to me: "Listen, you'd better let me handle these." I recognized the voice as my own. Immediately I was into myself again. I looked around me, bewildered to see myself there. Then I noticed that my hands were all bandaged up. I rushed in a panic to the washroom to find out what was wrong with them. The bandages were put on very sloppily, wound around and around. I said to myself: Come on, come on, look at it. I carefully unwound the gauze, and there underneath were a few little pinches and cuts that hardly needed a bandaid. I threw the bandages into the basin in a fury. Suddenly the scene at the beauty-parlor leapt back into my mind. I hadn't given a thought to it until that moment. At first I couldn't even believe I'd done it. A feeling of shame and hopelessness fell on me, as if someone had thrown a beachball to me and it had turned out to be filled with stones. I wandered back to my hilo in a daze, telling myself Margherita wouldn't look at me, she wouldn't bother to spit on me if I showed myself at our house again. What did I think I was doing by letting myself loose like I'd done, turning myself, who'd been a decent person, into some kind of a criminal? I didn't remember exactly what I'd done, but it must have been the stunts, and yelling at Margherita about her dresses, and I couldn't remember what else; hundreds of things. No wonder Margherita took a job. I felt that I'd crossed some boundary that I wouldn't be able to come back over again. I didn't know what I should do any more.

Our freight terminal was a building the size of two city blocks. It was completely open inside, like a gigantic barn. All along the four walls were garage-style doors which the trucks backed up to, to be loaded or unloaded. The lighter freight the dockmen moved around in carts, and the heavier freight we hilo-men handled. One corner of the terminal was screened off by a cage; here was where we put damaged or mislabeled freight. Some nights they'd race the hilos there. The section-supervisor in charge of the mislabeled-freight cage used to hide out for long periods in the washroom to read Superman comics. That's when the hilo-men would race.

Now the champion of the races was a heavy-set Irishman named Mickey Greenan, who always wore a baseball-cap backwards on his head, and who handled the hilo with a skill that nobody could match. He was a surgeon with those prongs; he could have parted your hair with them. He was also a union officer and very bitter against management. That night, he backed his hilo up to mine and challenged me to a race. I had never raced; I was afraid of getting fired. I told him no.

Ha ha ha, for him this was extremely funny, considering that business with the monsignor, like he always thought I was superstraight and regular since I wouldn't ever race, and now this, he said, and hey, he said, a lot of the guys are saying it must have been you, too, those priests who rowed across the river and got into the papers? And that woman you were with, wasn't she a knockout? What'd your wife think of that? And off he went to move some freight.

I was furious at him. He was obviously going around snickering to everyone about the mess I'd made of things. I'd only calmed down enough to get back to work when Greenan zipped past again: " 'Scuse me, Monsignor." A little while later he was back: "How's about that race, Father?" He kept going out of his way to torment me about his race, till finally I yelled at him that I'd do it, if he'd only shut up and leave me alone.

I didn't have enough time to think twice. Greenan had hardly finished shooting around announcing the race to his buddies when the section-supervisor of the racing-corner drifted by with a stack of Superman comic-books under his arm. In a minute we were up to the starting-mark. We each had a crate of four five-hundred-pound drums of solvent on our prongs: drums are harder to race with than solid freight, because the liquid tends to shift your balance on the turns. We were doing ten laps around the course for a dollar a yard at the finish line. Greenan gave me the inside lane to start and a quarter-lap as a handicap. I'd never raced before, and he assumed he'd win without any trouble. But I kept to the inside, and he couldn't pull ahead of me. By the fourth lap he began side-checking me — swinging up beside me and trying to shove me off the course.

The course had four sides. On two sides it ran between banks of empty loading-carts. That's where Greenan was side-checking me. On the other two sides, the race-course followed straight along the walls at the corner of the building. At any particular moment, some of the doors along the walls would be open to the backs of trucks. So the first rule of hilo-racing was never to side-check your opponent on the two sides of the course that followed along the walls. If someone was shoved off-course there, he might charge right through an open door onto the back of a truck and wreck the freight on it. Then there'd be hell to pay.

I broke this rule. I didn't forget about it; but we hadn't raced two laps when I figured out that I'd been had. Here I'd been feeling terrible about what I'd done, about the stunts and about going to jail and getting the monsignor fired and humiliating Margherita in front of everybody, and now what was I doing but getting involved in another crazy escapade that didn't even interest me and that might get me fired. With that, I thought, I'm supposed to obey rules made up by a joker like Greenan? I kept count, and every time he side-checked me legally, into the loading carts, I side-checked him illegally, towards the walls of the building. He fell behind a bit, and I could hear him there, cursing me at the top of his lungs. It never occurred to me to just drive out of the race. I was sold on the angry thought of beating him at his own game and collecting five or ten dollars to show him what I thought of him.

On the last lap he got his revenge. When you have a crate of drums up front on your prongs, the hilo makes a very good battering-ram. What Greenan must have planned was to ram me from behind, just before a turn, and send me barrelling through an open door into the back of a trailer. It would have meant some damage that I would have been blamed for. But one or two laps before the end, the truck pulled out that Greenan must have planned to ram me onto, so there was nothing outside the open door now but the asphalt parking lot outside the terminal, five feet below. I believe Greenan didn't notice that the truck had left. He probably was concentrating on getting his hilo right up behind mine. At the last turn of the race, he rammed me square, and I went sailing through the open door into the night.

As soon as I was clear of the walls, I jumped off the hilo and landed on the pavement below and rolled aside to get out of the way. I wasn't fast enough. The crate of drums slid off the the hilo-prongs and crashed onto my right leg and pinned me. The prongs stuck into the asphalt like a fork into a potato. The hilo shivered a bit, and then it started falling slowly down toward me.

I tugged and scratched and heaved in a frenzy at that crate of drums, trying to get it off my leg in time to drag myself away before the hilo could land on me. It seemed to be years. I raised myself up on my free foot in a sort of crouch, with the other leg all twisted and numb under the crate. I had the crazy idea I could lift the heavy crate off of me. I heaved, and up it came. I thought I was doing it myself: it was a miracle. Later Margherita told me that Greenan and some others had jumped down after me, and they had done the lifting. But I didn't see them, all straining as I was, and as the crate of drums came up off my leg, I felt a tremendous energy sweeping through my body and up through my mind. It was the same as I had felt it two weeks before, as I was getting out of the monsignor's limousine. I thought the energy was what had let me lift the crate off my leg, and not just the crate, but all the shame I'd been feeling, all the trouble with Margherita, and the stain of the past few years. When you put down a heavy weight that you've carried for a long distance, your arms feel suddenly light, as if they might almost float off: I felt that kind of lightness in my body. Everything around me seemed graced — the trucks parked in the lot, the men I saw running across the asphalt, the dark roof of the terminal against the sky, and the hilo falling and bouncing on the crates without making any noise. I thought to myself: I'm here. I don't remember anything more.

TWO

I WAS IN and out of surgery for two days while they patched up my shin-bone with steel pins and plastic. They never found all the old pieces. No one but Margherita and my parents and my sister came to visit me in the hospital. I asked Margherita where our friends were: hadn't she told them what had happened? She kept putting off an answer. Finally she said that Jimmy had called up to ask if it was true they were keeping me in the psycho-ward; he said if it was true, he wanted her to know that he was real sorry. She told him that it wasn't true, and after a while he did come over to the hospital to see me, but he treated me with a kind of sorrowful respect, and he got up to go almost as soon as he'd sat down. None of our other friends came at all. The monsignor stunt and the scene I'd made in the beauty-salon and the hilo-race and my smashing Margherita's dress-form, which soon enough in the gossip-circuit came to include the television set and most of the rest of our furniture, were more than enough to write me off as a mental case. They sent get-well cards and called up Margherita to ask if there was anything they could do.

I was very indignant about it. But lying there in traction and calming down and trying to look at what had happened, I had to admit it was natural for people to assume that there must be something wrong with me. As for myself, I didn't believe it. I'd gotten unnerved, that was all. The experience of the energy was too new; I told myself I'd gotten too excited, too exhilarated, and then I'd swung too far the other way afterward. Obviously the thing to do was not to touch the energy for a while, just leave it alone until I found someone like the monsignor to explain it to me and tell me how to handle it. There was no point in letting it disrupt my regular life.

"There aren't going to be any more problems, Margherita. Things are going back to normal." She visited me in the hospital every evening.

"You said that before, Joey," she told me. But both of us wanted to believe me.

"People are going to forget the whole thing like it never happened," I said. "As soon as the doctors let me out of this place, we're going around and visit with everyone, and they're going to see for themselves how my head is sitting right here on my neck and my hands are actually stuck on the ends of my arms, and what do you know? Joey answers to his name and he talks in sentences. They'll be wondering what all the fuss was about."

I remember she laughed like she always used to at ridiculous things I said. "Maybe we should hold off a little, though, Joey. Till things blow over."

"You think I am crazy, then?" I asked her. I was an expert at pushing her into a corner.

They let me out of the hospital on crutches on a Sunday, and two nights later we went off to our friends Tommy and Angela's house for dinner and canasta. This was a part of our routine, every third Tuesday of the month: in fact we held it on Tuesday because that was my night off. Angela is a niece of Margherita's brother-in-law Alfred, although they're about the same age. She's a very good Italian cook. Margherita called ahead to tell Angela that I was out of the hospital and we were coming, but you could tell once we got there that they weren't at all sure that I'd recovered. "How are you feeling, Joey?" the men all said with a very hearty note in their voices, as soon as we walked in the door.

"Never mind that," I said. "Just sign your name," and I stuck out the cast on my leg, which was covered with our son Vin's scribbles. The women avoided me and worried over Margherita. Tommy didn't offer me a beer, so I asked him for one, which made him nervous. "Sure, well, why not, I just thought maybe, with the doctors, your leg — hey, there's the door, maybe that's Bill and Mary Jo;" and he never gave me one. Bill and Mary Jo were a new couple in the group who we hadn't met before. He was an Irish guy from Tommy's job, and she was somebody's cousin. It was obvious they'd been invited in our place for the canasta hands. Neither of us ate much, especially Margherita, and the other women fussed over her and told her that she certainly ought to eat. They all had some relative or other who hadn't paid attention to her health during this or that bad time, and believe me, the weeks it took her to get back her strength, the medical bills —

The men were discussing the football season, which was about to begin. Football had never interested me, but normally I kept up my end of a conversation, even if I didn't know anything about the subject. In fact that was better; it allowed me to make ridiculous remarks. That night I couldn't see the point in it. I knew that this was wrong, since the whole point of our going there was for me to act my usual talkative self. But I couldn't bring it off. I told myself that if I've got to keep quiet about everything that's on my mind, why bother to say anything at all? The conversation just seemed like noise to me. I began wishing that the energy would come back again and slow things down and turn off the noise and make everything peaceful. I even tried concentrating my mind on being someone else so as to bring it on, but

I couldn't do it with the canasta-game going, and I kept losing track of the play. They'd have to remind me it was my turn. Finally I said that the new woman, Mary Jo, who was sitting out the game with Margherita, should maybe take my hand, because I was obviously not paying attention very well; I guessed I was tired. "Oh, yeah, sure, that's fine, Joey, that's all right," Tommy said. Everybody had a comment. "Yeah, sure, after an accident like that; sure, it takes a while to get going again; sure."

For dessert, Angela would usually make sfogliatelli; these are special Italian pastries that are eaten hot, with ricotta cheese in them. That night, when the cards were over and everyone was standing in the hall ready to go home, Angela brought out a couple of the pastries wrapped in aluminum foil and gave them to Margherita. "I always make a couple extra for Bethie and Marie," who were their kids, "but they aren't going to mind going without for once," she said. Margherita started biting her lip, and everybody looked on feeling pretty human. Suddenly I thought: hey, look, here's your chance to straighten people out a bit, particularly since you've probably been making a bad impression. So I said, more or less, "That's real nice of you, Angela. You don't have to worry about Margherita, though. Once I start getting around a bit better, I'm going to be cleaning up the house and taking care of Vin so long as I'm on disability — seeing as how she's working now and all." I hadn't actually told Margherita that; the thought had just struck me at that moment.

"That's real nice, Joey," everybody said. "Sure, you keep yourself busy."

"Just don't give her any pants to wear," said Bill, the new guy.

"That's right, that's right," the other men said, and everybody laughed.

"Besides," I said, "I felt pretty bad about messing up our place the other day, though actually, I don't know what you heard, but all I actually messed up was a thing or two of Margherita's in the bedroom. I was mad at her, which considering the circumstances was pretty wrong of me, but at least when you are mad it's better to bust up something somebody owns than to bust them up in person, am I right?" Everybody was falling all over themselves to agree with this, especially the women. "How's about it, Margherita, did you rather I'd broken your nose instead of your dress-form?"

It was as if I'd opened a window in the room in the direction of the breeze. Everybody was standing around talking all at once and recalling this or that time they'd gotten furious. I'd brought it off; I'd rescued my reputation with them. We should have left right then. But it was the same as with the monsignor stunt: I couldn't let a finished thing alone. I wanted to explain it all to them, so that they would understand. It was delighting me to have them standing around and laughing with me, thinking of me as good old Joey, the way they had before. Why shouldn't I share what I knew with them? They were my friends, weren't they? I didn't want to be an outcast.

There was a silence once people had done their recalling. So I told them: "The other thing, now, maybe you think those routines we did with the new monsignor in the parish were a little bit crazy, but" —

"Oh, yeah, I heard about that," the new guy Bill said. "That actually was you then?"

"It was laugh, it was a laugh, a once-in-a-lifetime thing, so let's forget about it," Tommy said.

"Yeah, sure, forget it," the men were saying. "Who cares?"

"No, okay," I said, "but there was something real in the things we did, besides just the fun and games. The way I felt in my mind while I was doing it, it was something very unusual, something you wouldn't ordinarily run into."

"Let's go home, Joey, all right? Joey?" Margherita said.

"No, I want to explain it to them. It's simple. If you change the way you act and you move into somebody else's type of shoes, your mind isn't going to have all the usual things to do, and so you

28

have a whole lot of extra energy all of a sudden." I'd just thought of this idea. I decided that I'd try to explain it all to them, step by step, so they'd be able to appreciate it. "So once there's this extra energy, it naturally starts building up, and pretty soon it's pouring up out of your mind, and all around you everything changes, and everything around looks beautiful."

They couldn't seem to see it yet. They were shifting their feet and looking at me with worried expressions on their faces. "Joey please, will you please?" Margherita said.

"I will, but look, I know I don't explain it very well, but just give me this much, Angela: if there could be this kind of energy"—

People were clearing their throats and saying it was late, they had to go. I didn't want them to. "Listen, there's nothing wrong in this, since if there is, then why was everything so beautiful?"

"Joey stop it, stop it," Margherita was saying.

"Okay, but should we just let it go and forget it?"

Tommy began loudly asking Mary Jo about her kids; they had just gotten over the measles.

"All right," I said, "I will stop, but if I am right, then you people should be worried about what you're missing. I just thought my friends might want to know about it."

Margherita was crying. People were saying good night to each other and going out the door.

"I was going to keep it to myself," I said. "You can pretend I didn't mention it, is that all right?"

The people who were still there looked up a second; there was a silence. "That's all right, Joey," Tommy said.

"That's all right, then?"

Everybody was leaving. Nobody answered. I tried to talk about football on the stairs.

For two months I sat around home, watching the quiz-shows and doing nothing and feeling confused. Sometimes I thought maybe my friends were right: the stunts had scrambled my brains. To make it worse, I found out, soon after that night at Tommy and Angela's, that I'd been fired from my job at the freight terminal. Greenan, the man I'd hilo-raced with, came over to the house to tell me about it. He said the company management hadn't technically fired me, since they couldn't actually prove I was hilo-racing — the supervisor had been reading comics in the washroom and everybody else who knew had clammed up; but they wanted me out, so they laid me off on the grounds that there were too many hilo-men on the floor. Greenan announced that they had another think coming if they thought they were getting away with this, since it was in violation of seniority rights and no-speed-up agreements and everything else. He was personally going to take it to grievance for me. All I had to do, Joey pal, was sign these papers here. I signed them and more or less forgot about it. With disability pay and Margherita's salary, more money was coming in than before, so for the time being I didn't have to worry about keeping up. I just wanted to rest and someday begin my life again.

After about ten weeks, the doctors said my leg had knit. They took off the last of a series of casts and told me my therapy was to walk. I used to go out every day twice with Vin, who was just starting to walk for distances himself. He was a little over three then. We'd walk down the back streets together or take a bus to North Hudson Park in North Bergen, or we'd pick around the Hoboken piers. I'd put him on my shoulders when he got tired.

It was autumn then. Day after day there was clear air and a blue sky, and everything was bright in the sun, even the faded bricks of the old knitting mills. I taught Vin the colors as we went, and a lot of the names of things. He knew all the cars. "Tazin ragon," he called it. "Frord." One day we were walking on the grounds of Stevens Institute, a technical college in Hoboken. Between the old physics building there and the piers on the Hudson River nearby, there's an acre or two of very large old trees. You walk under a roof of high-up branches and leaves. That day a wind came up off the Hudson, and the leaves, which were pale green and tan and bright yellow with the fall, started trembling and flipping very fast back and forth all through the branches over us with a tremendous hiss. The dying leaves rained down on us. All of a sudden I could tell that the energy had come back again. I could feel it physically: a silent buzzing that was piling up under the top of my scalp. I thought that in a minute it would be strong enough to push my mind open and stream out into the air, the way it had before. I didn't want my mind to open; I didn't want any of it. I was afraid that it would be stronger than I could control, that it would pour out everywhere and make everything tremble, not just the leaves but the ground and the buildings and Vin too, and myself, everything would tremble into that yellow autumn sunlight and dissolve away in a hiss. I thought I might lose myself and not be able to find myself afterward. I tried to stop the energy by standing still and looking at the ground and trying to think the silent buzzing down into my body. It seemed to work. The buzzing slowly sank down below my chest and was absorbed. After a minute or two, the wind from the river died down, and the leaves were still. When we went home on the bus I was feeling pretty shaken.

That night I dreamed that I was wading in a brook; it was a summer evening. A homemade dam just a little downstream held up the water in a clear pool around me, and the current went on past me up to my waist in some places, sometimes just up to my knees. There were trees leaning over the banks, and smooth pebbles were on the bottom. Though it was dark out, I could see down through the water, and there around my legs some fish maybe a foot long were swimming back and forth and nibbling at my legs, as they will sometimes in streams. Their scales were full of bright streaks of green and yellow and tan like the leaves in Hoboken; I remember noticing that in the dream.

The fish were talking — it was a dream; and I could under-stand them. There weren't any actual spoken words. What they said just sounded up to me, in a kind of high-pitched singing. They were telling me about the energy piling up in my mind and waiting to pour out; they told me what would happen if I calmed down and let it pour, and how I would see new things. They said I was changing in the way I'd changed a thousand times before, times I had forgotten; they said I didn't have to be afraid. I understood everything. A tremendous feeling of kindness and gentleness washed up from their singing and from the way they nibbled on my skin and from the flashes of the colors of their scales. It spread up through the current of the stream and up into the trees and the air. Everything was solved. I woke up and fell asleep and dreamed it again, and then again.

I spent the next morning trying to get back into my mind what the fish had told me — what it was that I had known. I never remembered; but for days afterward I had that feeling you can get from a strong dream, of another life soaking through your own. I believed what I had dreamed. I told myself: see, it's right, what's going to happen; I don't care what Tommy and Angela say. I don't care if I am a mental case. Next time the energy comes, it can pour where it wants. But then nothing happened for a couple of weeks, and for a while I thought it was over.

Then one afternoon near a drinking-fountain in North Hudson Park, Vin slipped on the wet slick pavement and scraped his knee. It wasn't much of a wound, although I guess it stung, but I made a big production of it: ripping my handkerchief in strips, soaking one strip in the fountain to wash his knee, and wrapping the other strips around for a bandage, telling him how we both had bad legs now — like other kids, he'd suddenly forget he'd been crying, and he'd start staring at what you were doing, with his face all wet. It was that way with the bandage; we became very absorbed in it. While I was concentrating on knotting it up a final time, suddenly the energy was buzzing silently in my scalp again. It ran in a straight thin line underneath my skin from the bridge of my nose back across the top of my head and down to the nape of my neck. I was afraid; but I told myself, no, be quiet; let it happen. When we got up to walk again, the silent buzzing began to spread down the sides of my head and into my shoulders and then all the way down my body, just underneath my skin. As it built up strength, it began radiating outward from my body, it seemed from all my pores, as if it was an invisible kind of light. I felt larger. I tried to keep my thoughts on the fish in the dream, in order to stay calm. The energy grew; I felt I was burning. But no heat was in the fire. Instead it cooled me from the heat of the warm day. The energy seemed to burn up my physical boundaries till I couldn't feel my clothes or tell one part of my body from the other or tell where my skin bordered on the air.

All around us in the sunlight, the park was clearer and brighter. The flowing of the energy had changed my way of seeing, and I thought that the act of seeing itself must be a kind of light, and that its frequency could be increased from within. As I watched, everything in the park seemed to move slower and grow quieter — the children running in the grass and their mothers and their dogs and the wind — so that all hardly moved and their voices dimmed out to a trace: you might have thought that the park was under water. But the water was as empty and as peaceful as space, and perfectly clear and still. The same stillness was in myself. I knew where I was, and my thoughts ran on as before, but below my mind, my body felt continuous with the quietness of the air. Everything seemed resolved. Within me and outside, there was no tension, no opposition, no plans, and no fear.

I looked down at Vin, thinking I'd ask him if he felt anything strange. Walking there next to me, with his little feet zipping out in front, one then the other, trotting for a second to keep pace, he seemed perfect to me: the only child in the park. Everything around him had receded behind, as if it was only scenery. Then I noticed that if I looked at something else than him, a bench, the grass, a piece of paper, even, then it too would silently bloom, like a lamp turned on in a room in the late afternoon.

When it did bloom, though, all the while that it was perfect, I could see how caught it was being itself; how the drinking-fountain was completely shut into being a fountain, so that it could never be the little black girl drinking from it or the water dripping down it at the sides. Suddenly this seemed liked a terrible thing to me, that none of the people and the things could change. I felt myself, too, stuck like the little girl and the fountain, hammered down by spikes into my ankles and my shoulders, a machine that couldn't do any other thing that what it was made to do. Again and again I felt a wave of desire to change from what I was. I wanted to drop everything in my life so that I could turn my body and all my thoughts and feelings into the energy pouring out of me. I wanted to pour out into the stillness around me and never return.

For the next month and a half, all through the fall while my leg regained its strength, I practiced concentrating my mind on whatever I was doing, the way I'd concentrated on Vin's bandage by the fountain, or on lifting the crate of drums off my leg the night of the accident. I decided it was concentration that made the energy build up and pour out and leave me feeling still and clean. The stunts were no longer needed. They had just been a cumbersome method of concentration that I'd happened to stumble on. Now the energy came whatever I concentrated on, though it varied in strength, depending on how quiet I felt in my emotions. It was only long afterwards that I understood what it had actually meant to try to escape my ordinary self the way I'd done in the stunts, and why the energy had begun to be revealed at the moment when I'd begun, though at first just in play, to ask myself who I was.

When Magherita was at work and Vin and I weren't walking, I spent my time working on the car or cleaning up the house. I learned how to cook and to look after all the details of raising a child. I understood why women get into the state where all they talk about is children. Cleaning Vin and touching him and watching him and hearing him filled my mind till I believe that even now, if I had the skill, I could make a plaster cast of him from memory as he was then, down to the last wrinkle. We had a washing-machine completely paid for, but I took to washing his clothes by hand, and Margherita's clothes and mine too: anything to concentrate my mind. It was far past being just a game now. I didn't know where the experience of the energy was pushing me, but I knew now that from the beginning it had been taking me out of my old life. I was glad. The life of West New York no longer interested me. I'd pass our women friends in the street or see them in the grocery store — hi, how are you, fine, how's Margherita — I didn't care if I ever saw them again. There was going to be something else than the old life; I didn't know what, but it was going to be fine. I was going to understand. Maybe I'd look up the monsignor, to ask him to explain what was happening to me; maybe everything would come clear soon, of its own accord. As soon as I'd understood, I'd teach the energy to Margherita and Vin; it would make Vin smart; someday he'd go to college. Pretty soon now we'd be moving to a new place, maybe to the country. We'd find better jobs and a house with a yard and new friends.

I didn't tell Margherita about these daydreams. I was afraid she wouldn't understand yet. But she did see how much calmer I was, and she didn't question me. For the first time in a long while, we were happy together.

Sometimes uneasiness would take hold of me. I'd be in the midst of cooking or washing the dishes or crawling around cleaning, and my mind would stray off into thoughts about what all the people I knew must be saying about me. I'd think of them talking about how I was avoiding them, how I was staying home and doing women's jobs; how I'd gone off the deep end. Then I'd think they all were right: something horrible had happened to me, something frightening. I was losing myself; I would never be normal again; I would end up on a mental ward. A kind of panic would come over me. I'd have to bite down hard on my lip and try to put away quietly the cleaning-tools or whatever it was that I was doing, and then I'd sit away the rest of the day in front of the television quiz-shows, hoping I could calm down before Margherita came home. But she always could tell. The panics came more and more often. We both were worried about it, although neither of us mentioned it.

One morning in October, Greenan and two of the paid officers from the union local came over to talk to me. I didn't hear them on the stairs. I was on my hands and knees, concentrating on putting wax down evenly on the floor of the hall. The front door was open for the cleaning. The three men barged on through, calling out for me, and the first one walked into the mop which was sticking up out of a pail of dirty water by the door. Splosh, the pailful slopped down the hall over the wet wax to where I was kneeling. With my pants all dripping, I leapt up in a fright, the way people will when they're caught at something they don't what to be seen doing. Immediately I was yelling at the three men at the top of my voice. "Who are you coming in here wrecking my place like you own it? I'm in here peaceful by myself not bothering anybody, and you've got to come in and mess things up like this" —

Greenan and his union friends didn't know what to make of it. Here was this madman in bare feet and a flowery apron and an old felt hat on his head and his hands full of rags: they decided to joke their way out of it. "Hey, listen, Joey," Greenan said, "We ought to get you into grievance-work yourself. You'd have them shaking so hard they'd sign anything."

"You get out of here! You get out of here!" I was yelling, and I was shivering as if the spilled water had given me a chill.

"Okay, Joey, okay." They backed out, their soaked shoes sloshing in the water. "We just wanted to tell you we got shot down on your grievance, so maybe you'd okay an appeal?"

"No I don't want an appeal, why should I want to work in

that garbage dump full of you creeps?" I was crying with confusion and rage. Greenan came back in, challenging me to repeat that, but the union men yelled at him, and one got hold of his arm, and after a minute they went away.

I sat there on the upturned pail, trying to keep still. I felt shaken as if I had vomited. Greenan's voice was down there on the street; they were obviously talking about me. I began imagining his union friends telling their wives about me and their wives having concerned faces, and Greenan telling his buddies at the terminal, and them shrugging their shoulders and laughing. Joey's just crazy, he's crazy; pictures shot up into my mind of different people saying that, with sad or amused or bewildered or scornful expressions on their faces. The pictures flashed at me one after the other very fast, as if a reel of film was being yanked through my head. If they see how I clean up, I thought, then they won't be saying that, and I began wandering through the house, putting things in different places and moving lamps and knick-knacks around without keeping track of what I was doing. I was arguing in my thoughts with the supervisor of the hilo-racing corner about how he shouldn't let the racing go on the way he did, and then Greenan was in the argument and the police commissioner and Bohanian the lawyer and Cinderella, all arguing at once till my mind was full of shouting. More and more people crowded into the argument, each one making moral observations about what I'd been doing — my father, my mother, my sister Donna, Tommy and Angela, the new monsignor, all making sober observations about how serious this was and how Joey ought to reform, till my head was stuffed with the blabbing of it. I thought it would pack itself in till the sides of my mind would crack open under the pressure and all my thoughts would burst out like hornets from a torn nest. I wanted to run downstairs to where Margherita's sister Carmella was with her kids and with Vin, so that her talking would put something else into my mind, but the idea of doing it wouldn't stay still long enough for me to remember what it was that I'd decided to do. As I wandered around the house, what I saw with my eyes became mixed with the pictures in my mind till I forgot there was a difference, and the blabbing filled up the rooms.

Slowly it quieted down, as one by one the blabbing people left. It seemed like they stepped backwards out the windows and the doors of the room that I was in. I couldn't remember if they all had actually been there in the room, or if the room was my mind. I tried to think which, but immediately I forgot what I was thinking about. Broken bits of pictures and stray words were wandering upward in the air, just out of reach along the walls, not staying long enough for me to look at them or listen to them. They floated past and up through the ceiling. They came up faster and each one fainter till they were blowing all around in a garbled mist full of colors and vague sounds. After a while they were gone. I looked around: there were no thoughts. The room was empty, and it had no ceiling or walls. There were no sounds anywhere and no shapes and no light, and I lost my body in the darkness. There was nothing at all except a small place of knowing that there was nothing. Suddenly I knew that that place, too, would be taken. A feeling of damp chill began to grow at me from everywhere around me: it seemed to fill up the darkness. I knew that when it reached me it would swallow that last place in myself, so that I would never know anything again. I was terrified till I was nothing but the terror.

Suddenly I felt something else: something warm. I tried to find where it was so I could go to it and escape. The thought came that the warmth was on my face; it was around my head. At first I didn't know what that meant. Then suddenly it hit me that I must be a person; if I had a face, I must be a person. I wasn't sure about it, but I scrambled at it anyway: anything to escape. I tried to think of everything I knew about being a person: a body, and other people, hard things to touch, being in one place at a time — pictures and voices slowly began to rise out of the darkness, more and more of them coming faster and faster till they spilled over themselves like the water of a fountain, and the air was alive with a shower of bright colors and sounds. Then I noticed the shapes were all outside me, and I was among them.Margheritawas there. We were sitting on the floor of our kitchen, and she was holding my head in her arms.

I held onto her for a long while. The chill left; the dark emptiness was gone.

"Joey? Joey, are you all right?"

I waited another few moments, than sat back by myself, nodding.

"Carmella called me at work, she heard you shouting at those men."

"Those" — it took me a second to get my voice. "What men is this?"

"They came up here, she said you sounded terrible" —

It came back to me then, how the thing started.

"Union guys. The grievance didn't make it."

"The grievance?" She was squatting behind me and embracing me again, with her face next to mine. " Joey, what happened? What happened to you? You were sitting here just shouting and shouting like somebody was attacking you, and you didn't even hear me talk to you, you didn't even hear me."

"I felt you, Margherita." I looked at her arm bent around in front of me, with the watch on it and fine hairs and the smooth skin; I thought it was something I never wanted to let go of.

"Why didn't you hear me, Joey?"

"I don't know, Margherita. A lot of blabbing thoughts came in and took over my head, and I couldn't hear anything. I didn't know where I was."

"How does this happen? I don't understand how this happens?"

"I don't understand either. How am I supposed to understand?"

"Okay, Joey. It's okay now."

She came around and squatted down in front of me, looking very concerned, and dressed very spiffily for work, in a blue-grey blouse and dark blue skirt, with her hair carefully fixed. I felt proud of her. "You look real fine, Margherita."

"Can't you tell me anything, Joey?"

"I don't know, except it was like the other time, when I smashed up your dress-form, but this time I was awake, and I had to watch it all. I got angry, and then my mind emptied out till there weren't any thoughts left in it. It felt like there was darkness all round, and I got lost."

She had a very worried look and was biting her lip. But she didn't say anything.

The furniture and appliances in the kitchen seemed a little new and strange, the way things seem after you've been sick a long while. "Did I break anything in the house?" I asked her.

"No, just a couple things, I didn't look" —

"I want to see." I got up and started for the swinging door to the living-room.

"No wait," she said. She stood up and looked at me, still biting her lip. "Wait here a second, okay, Joey?"

I thought she was afraid I'd get upset again when I saw what I'd done. "I messed up, did I?"

"No — just wait a minute?"

"Yeah, sure, Margherita."

She edged herself out the door so I wouldn't see what was beyond it, and suddenly there was whispering and shushing. I recognized Carmella's whisper, and there was a man: it was my father. I guessed Carmella had called him, too, to protect the women in case I went wild. It suddenly hit me that Margherita must have become frightened of me. Long afterwards, looking back on it, I realized that she'd always been frightened of me.

My father and Carmella left; the front door closed quietly. Margherita came back into the kitchen, giving me that nervous wary look again, as if she thought I'd be angry at her for having them there. For the first time in all those months, I felt sorry for her.

We went into the other rooms. The telephone and two or three chairs were knocked over, and a lamp was broken; that was all. I sat down on the sofa, deciding that I owed it to her to tell her what I knew. "See, the thing is, Margherita, in the good times, there's some kind of energy that pours out of my mind, and I feel all filled with a clear and peaceful feeling; everything around me is clear and peaceful — I feel like finally I almost understand what it's supposed to mean to be alive. Did you ever feel that? Then in the bad times, it's just the opposite: the more my mind pours out, the emptier it gets, and everything is angry and frightening. This is what happened today. I thought I was going to die, although I guess I wouldn't have; I don't know."

"Why do you do it, then? Joey why do you do this?"

"I don't do it, Margherita. It happens to me. I admit that I've been looking for the good times, but this is just so I can understand it, and use it, maybe — I didn't ask for this, Margherita. It's some kind of force that got hold of me somewhere, and it's pushing me and pushing me."

She was sitting on the floor in front of me, leaning against me. "You got to get help, don't you know that?"

"Who is going to understand, though? Who is going to know about this? If I mention it to anybody, they think I'm crazy."

"There are doctors, Joey. You aren't the only person in the world who gets upset."

"Yes, but doctors are for when you're crazy, and I don't think that craziness is what this is; that's what I'm trying to tell you, Margherita."

"You don't know what's wrong with you, Joey," she said. "Maybe there's some infection from your accident or your operation, maybe it's something mental they've got pills for, we don't know, and how are we ever going to know if we don't try?"

"Yeah, okay, I can see this, but doctors, Margherita — I've been thinking I should maybe try to find out where the new monsignor went."

I could feel her stiffen up. "Why him, though, Joey? Why do you think he's going to tell you anything? Just because he invited you over that day? He's a priest, all he knows about is the Church."

"Okay, he's a priest, but priests sometimes talk about people seeing things." She looked up at me quickly, almost angrily. "All right, maybe you think that's just what's crazy," I said. "But if it is crazy, why is it beautiful, Margherita? That's what you still haven't explained. If it wasn't beautiful, do you think I'd care two seconds about it? If it didn't feel right and peaceful? What if you saw the most beautiful, I don't know what, the most beautiful lake, and there was a dock there with a sign on it saying: 'No Trespassing and Absolutely No Swimming in Here,' but everything was peaceful and still, and there was no one around but me and Vin, no one anywhere around, wouldn't you want to take off your clothes right there and swim? I know how you like to swim, Margherita."

"I don't know what I'd do, Joey." She was standing in front of me and looking down on me very steadily. "But that's swimming or not swimming. This is going crazy or not going crazy. You've got to see a doctor."

"Yeah, okay. I can see this: okay. Except can I go see the monsignor too, though? if I can find him? We'll try both, Margherita?"

I think this was when she started to move away from me in her mind, out of self-defense. "Okay, Joey. We'll try both."

THREE

WHAT WAS I to say to a psychiatrist? We got the appointment
through Margherita's uncle, and so of course I was suspicious of
the doctor before I even saw him. His office was off Journal
Square in Jersey City, in a made-over wooden house painted blue;
the house had one of those round turrets sprouting from the roof.
Windows lined the office half around, and as you faced the doctor
you looked out on a back garden full of wisteria vines. Fouchaud,
his name was: he had a fancy wide tie and a big moustache and a
constant smile around his eyes, like he'd had a good weekend and
a good lunch and was looking forward to a good dinner, too, with
another very definitely good weekend coming up starting Friday
at 3:00 p.m. sharp. "How do you feel now?" he asked me, as soon
as we'd introduced ourselves.

"Yeah, well, I don't know; Margherita, Margherita that's my
wife, she thinks maybe I got some poison in me that's causing
this."

"Is that what you think?" he said, very pleasantly.

"How should I know? You're the doctor."

"We'll do some tests. But what do you think?"

I was feeling pretty stubborn, but I'd told myself on the way there on the bus that I was going to keep at least this promise, since I hadn't kept any of the others. "I'll do whatever you say, as long as it doesn't get too expensive."

He held up his watch to show me. It had one of those wide leather bands. "It'll cost you fifty cents a minute to tell me what you think is wrong, and fifty cents a minute to beat around the bush. Okay?"

"Yeah, if that's how you want it. All right. I don't think there's probably any poison. I think maybe I'm crazy like people say, but it certainly isn't what I used to think was meant by crazy. Sometimes my mind goes wrong on me, and if you give me something to stop it going wrong or at least to tone it down some, I'll pay you a dollar a minute and I'll thank Mr. Rossi for sending me here" — he was Margherita's uncle— "though that would hurt, believe me."

"Tell me what happens when your mind goes wrong on you."

"This is what I'm here about. Didn't somebody tell you?"

"No one told me."

"Well — no one told you?"

"No."

"Well, my mind emptied out." I told him about what had happened the week before, and I have to say he forgot about his weekends and leaned forward and listened pretty carefully. He kept asking me at each part: "And how did you feel about it?" I hadn't wanted to tell him about the stunts and the energy pouring out, but he eased that out of me, too. He hadn't gone to school for ten years for nothing. I told him I didn't want to be cured of the energy.

"What you want," he said after I'd finished, "is to let your mind go out of control and let it go where it wants when it's acting pleasantly, but to keep it under control when it's acting unpleasantly."

"Maybe, I guess."

"And you think there might be a pill for that?" he said.

"I don't know; is there?" For a minute I thought he was going to help me out. "If you gave it to me, Margherita would kick herself around the block for suggesting this."

"Listen, Joey," he said. "If you let a dog out, you can't tell what he'll do. He'll go where he wants. Maybe he'll have a good time with a bitch in heat or a woodchuck; maybe he'll get splattered all over the road by a truck. You can't give him a pill to stop one and not the other. The only way to stop him from being run over once is to keep him at home all the time."

"You're telling me I've got to keep the lid on."

"What do you think?"

"I'll bet you got pills for that all right."

"Yes, we do. Temporarily. There are tranquilizers which can keep you on an even keel while you work on learning how to keep your mind and your feelings within bounds on your own. If that's what we decide."

"You mean I have to agree to it?"

"If you want help, Joey, I think you probably can get help. What you actually do is up to you."

He was pushing me into a corner, the same as Margherita and our friends had; except that he was an expert at it. This was obviously what Margherita had hoped for. But his tranquilizers seemed to me like some kind of burial.

"What I don't understand," I told him, "is why everybody just assumes that the whole thing is wrong and crazy, when they don't even know what it is. I mean you haven't told me what the energy is, Doctor, because maybe you don't even know, and neither do I, all right?" I was working myself up into a fit of indignation. "Maybe the reason I go wrong in this thing is that I don't understand it and I don't know what I'm doing. It's like working with electricity, see? If you don't know what you're doing, you can get thrown across the room. Now why isn't that just as good a theory as the theory that the whole thing is crazy?"

He was leaning forward very intently. "We can explore this thing and find out about it as we work together, Joey. People have thought about what happens in the mind; it doesn't have to be a mystery. But meanwhile you're flirting with throwing your mind away, and I don't think you can afford to do it. I think it's dangerous. You have too much at stake."

"That's right, I have everything at stake, but what is this everything? It's going to a job five nights a week and playing canasta every second Tuesday with people who think I'm a mental case, and it's hoping I can save up enough for a one-family house, and wishing I could own a fuel-oil-delivery business and a weekend cabin in the Delaware Gap, that's the 'everything' you're talking about, Doctor. That's what my life meant before the energy started, and the cure you're supposed to give me is to make me want it all back." The words were rushing out of me and I felt hot in my face with pity for myself. "I could have thrown my mind away five years ago for all the good it was doing me then. Maybe I didn't used to think that, but now it's too late, that's what Margherita can't see, it's too late, so she might as well stop fighting me and start helping me out."

The doctor sat there frowning to himself. The hour was up. He asked me if I could tell when a bad spell was coming on. "I get nervous more often; it builds up," I said. He wrote me a prescription. "These will calm you down when you get nervous." After I'd left his office, I bought the pills, in order to have something to show Margherita; but for a long time I never took them. I didn't want them to influence my mind.

I went to a clinic for two days' worth of tests: blood-sugar, urine, spinal tap, brain-waves. They were looking for diabetes, a tumor, a hormonal upset, cancer even. They found nothing. Margherita was relieved and also fearful, because now it looked like my problem had to be psychological.

As for myself, I assumed the tests had vindicated me. I wasn't sick; whatever was happening to me was genuinely in my mind, just as I'd believed. I told this to the psychiatrist when I went back to him for another session. He said he wasn't actually surprised that the tests didn't show anything, because he'd also suspected that my problem was a mental one. If I cooperated, he believed I could be cured.

I told him I didn't want to be cured. I just wanted to understand.

"Curing will come from understanding, Joey."

"You say that because you see what's happened to me as a problem, Doctor, but I see it as a lucky chance, see what I mean? When you got the chance to go to medical school, would you have listened to anyone who told you it was a problem?"

"I wanted to be a psychiatrist," he said. "That's where I was going. What do you want to be, Joey? Where are you going?"

He was looking at me intently; he thought he had me, and he was right: I couldn't answer him. But I believed there was an answer, and I believed that I would find it, if only I could find out where to look. I couldn't be persuaded I was crazy, although to everybody else this was more and more the obvious explanation. But I always had a stubborn nature. Even when I was a kid, I'd trusted my own mind above everything, and by now the energy had given me too much delight, and the feeling of it was too right, for me to let myself be pushed back, whatever the trouble I was in.

I kept thinking of the monsignor staring at me the first moment that I'd felt the energy, when I was getting out of his limousine. I started wondering the same thing I had wondered back then: if there mightn't be a religious explanation. It's not that I thought I'd been chosen by the saints, or I'd received the call or anything like that. I didn't believe in the saints, or in God or Jesus either. From the very first, I'd had the idea that I'd stumbled on something that was probably pretty common and open to everyone. This is why I'd wanted my friends to know about it. Hadn't the monsignor recognized what I was feeling? Hadn't he told me when he'd dropped me off at home: "Come and see me"? It was time to go find him.

I took the tube to Newark to the archdiocese headquarters to see if they knew where he was. Inside, thin young priests, surrounded by panelled walls, sat behind desks under chandeliers. One after the other they told me that there was no priest by that name in this archdiocese.

"Okay, but he was here four months ago."

"I don't know about that. For that you'll have to ask Father So-and-So, second floor, turn to your left."

The elevator had thick wooden doors with large crosses carved in them. I rode from floor to floor with priests who carried briefcases and wore wire-rimmed glasses and discussed business. Finally a young sister on the top floor went into the back room and came out again grinning and waving a file-folder above her head. "Believe it or not," she said, "I found the man, which could be classified as a miracle. He joined the Carmelite Fathers and is living in a monastery near Cheshire, Massachusetts."

The monsignor had become a monk.

"You got to be kidding."

"Nope," she said.

I wrote him a letter: "Dear Father Jeremy (this was the Carmelite name he had taken): You said I should come see you, and now I hope you'll let me. There's something I have to ask you. By the way, they sold the parish limo."

He wrote back right away on a postcard: "You're welcome to come. What day do you propose?" There was a postscript which said: "It was all for nothing. I never got my Peugeot."

I could tell that Margherita was suspicious about my going. She thought I was running after another one of my crazy ideas, when I ought to be buckling down and shaping up and getting cured. I told her there was no harm in trying every angle, and anyway it would only be for three or four days. "You probably forgot what a relief it was to have me out of the house, Margherita."

Next day there was another postcard from the monsignor — from Father Jeremy. A brother at his monastery, named Stephen, was visiting his parents in Hackensack, which isn't far from West New York; Father Jeremy suggested that Brother Stephen might drive me to the monastery on his way back. I called him. "If Father Jeremy says this is okay, I take you," said Brother Stephen in a very noticeable accent which I took to be German. "You don't mind paying the tolls, of course," the brother said.

The next Friday I took the bus to Hackensack, feeling pretty hopeful. At the last minute before I left, Margherita got very worried and asked me to wait a little longer before I went. But I told her there was no problem; I had the tranquilizers. Vin was already down at Carmella's. I told myself, why bother getting into a discussion with Carmella? So I didn't go in to say goodbye to Vin. In later times, my mind went back to that and back to that to regret it.

The street where Brother Stephen's parents lived was lined with narrow three-story houses with peaked roofs and large banks of front steps: the kind of working-people's street with old trees where they'd rather see a tornado strike than see a colored person getting out of a decent-looking car with the classified section of the newspaper in his hand. Brother Stephen was at the door; he didn't invite me in. He was a broad-shouldered man over six feet tall, with very light blond hair, even on his eyelashes. He wore long brown robes and a filigree gold cross that swung on a chain from his rope-cincture. He couldn't have been more than twenty-one. "You are Father Jeremy's friend?" he said.

"Yes, Brother, that's right."

"We are going." He led me to a broken-down old Ford Mustang parked in the driveway, and after stalling it a couple of times, he got it started and said: "Please pay me for the tolls now. It is three dollars and twenty-five cents."

"Yeah, okay, but look, Brother, I've been looking at the road-map" — in fact I'd had it out twenty times in the past week, to day-dream over it — "and if you'll let me show you" — I opened the map and showed him how we could get to Massachusetts through New York State instead of Connecticut, and avoid most of the tolls on a route that was shorter.

"There are many hills this way," he said.

"I'll drive that part if you don't like them," I told him.

He frowned a minute, and then suddenly his face flushed very red and he jammed the car in gear and roared out of the place. I thought to myself: well, one nut deserves another; this is going to be some trip. But he went up into New York State as I'd suggested, and he didn't say a word the whole morning.

We stopped for lunch at a turnpike cafeteria. "Please eat," Brother Stephen said as we went through the line. "I am paying for you." He must have seen how much that surprised me, so he added, muttering it: "This tolls matter was very stupid of me."

"Hey, no," I said, "I'm sorry I forced myself on you."

"Force?" he said. "I have Father Jeremy to thank for sending you."

"Yeah?" I didn't know what to make of him. Over the food he completely loosened up and breezed on about this and that, how his sister was pregnant again and his parents were moving to a mobile home park in Florida, meanwhile stuffing himself with beef and potatoes and flashing smiles which made him look three or four years younger, just a clean-cut kid turned eighteen.

Later on in the car we began talking again, and I asked him how he happened to become a brother — not expecting much of an answer. But he seemed to want to talk about himself, and he told me his story. He said he'd come over from the other side, from Europe, when he was fifteen, and he went to a high school in Hackensack. In his senior year he took up steady with a girl, but after graduation she wouldn't marry him. "She said I am a tight-fisted Tcherman."

"You aren't, particularly, Brother," I told him. "You've just got careful instincts, is all."

"I am *Swedish*," he said, but instead of being offended, he laughed very loudly and delightedly, which made him take his eyes off the road and nearly sideswipe somebody. He wasn't a very good driver.

Of course the girl was right about him, he said. He had the peculiarity of always being afraid that things would be taken from him. When he went up to the blackboard in class or out to recess, for example, he'd take his books along with him, in case someone stole them. Naturally, there was soon enough a group of wiseacres who took to hiding his briefcase and pencils and hat and coat, just for the laugh of seeing him frantic over it. After a while, he was handcuffing his briefcase to his wrist wherever he went. Once he had graduated, he went to work in a shoe-factory. His problem got worse. He mounted a series of elaborate locks on the doors and windows of his parents' house, the kind they mount on the entrances to commercial establishments. It got so that he had to check and recheck the locks five times over to make sure they were fast before he could go off to work or get to sleep at night.

"I wanted to reform, believe me I did," Brother Stephen told me. "I said to my girl friend, 'Please, give me a chance.' But I couldn't change. I would lie there in bed and think about that back door; was it locked, are you sure? Certainly I was sure, I'd checked it only ten minutes back; but I wasn't sure, and I'd drag myself up out of bed and check the back door, and also check all the other ones just in case. 'Christ in Heaven, aren't you asleep?' my mother would call out — I drove her to blasphemy. I took no lunch to my work in the shoe-factory, because who could tell if my lunch pail would disappear? I knew it was all foolishness. But I couldn't silence my doubting and my fears. Many times I asked myself: 'What is it that gives me this? It is someone controlling me, perhaps?' I wondered if I had a devil. Could it be? I began to go to Mass; I prayed to God. 'If this is a devil, take it away, please, God.' I confessed to my sins, all of them, every one; I made up new ones to confess and then confessed that. But I never mentioned the locks to the confessor. I couldn't bear the idea of a venerable Father laughing at me the way my girl-friend had laughed when I told her about the devil. She sat down on the front steps and laughed till she cried and walked away down the street laughing till she was out of sight. Nothing helped. I put on more locks and more; I believed I was damned. There was no sleep. My head burned. At last my poor parents had me committed to an insane asylum.

"It was a hospital of the Sisters of Mercy, may God bless all of them. A priest came around hearing confessions. Many sinners are saved in such hospitals. I thought to myself: this father has heard very many insanities; perhaps he will not laugh at mine. I told him about my lock-devil. 'You cannot help, Father,' I said. 'I am damned.'

" 'No one is damned if he repents,' the father replied.

"I reproached him: 'But I have repented of everything, and the devil is still here.'

" 'Have you repented of this devil?' the father asked.

" 'That's for it to do! I can't make him.'

" 'It is your devil, my son. You have accepted him as yours. It's a sin to accept a devil and to turn away from your family and from yourself and from God for the sake of such a thing.'

"I was astonished at what he said, even angry. 'How can you say that the devil is my sin?' I asked him. 'It's not mine. I don't want it.'

" 'If you don't want it,' this quick-minded father said, 'give it to God, and he will deal with it. Commit yourself to God, and tell him you're sorry.'

"I was even more astonished, and I burst into tears.

" 'Tell God you're sorry,' the father said, 'and he will forgive you.' And he said the absolution."

It was so simple it was laughable: the Swede could actually become some one else than the lock-fanatic of Van Steuben Street. He sat there on his hospital bed in a daze at the idea. He'd just consign the devil and the locks to God. It hit him that he was exhausted; he slept for two days. When he woke up, he thought the devil had gone. God had taken it. Relief spread through him, he said, like the scent of a rose. They let him out of the hospital and he walked the whole way home, feeling like he didn't weigh anything, like the whole city didn't weigh a pound, like everything in it was ready to float away and disappear at the touch of a feather; he wouldn't have cared. When he got home, he dismantled all the locks and opened wide all the doors and windows in the place, so when his mother came in, she nearly had a heart attack.

"So now that you were fixed up like the girl wanted," I asked him, "you decided not to get married after all?"

"Fixed up, I was?" He laughed his delighted loud laugh. "I had to sleep, and how could I sleep without locks? Yes, I had given the devil to God, but perhaps God had given it back to me? I was waking one night, two nights, three nights. Every sound on the street, every creak in the house was a knife in my heart. Without locks, I thought the house would collapse on me. On the third night near morning, I began mounting locks on the doors again. My mother sobbed, my father in his bedclothes was shouting and hit me. It was as if I heard nothing and felt nothing. They called for the straightjacket, but by the time they came with it, it was not needed. The locks were back on, and I was sitting among the tools, weeping like a frightened child.

"The wise father at the hospital scolded me. 'You cannot take all the locks off at once, my son. The miracles of God only appear to come suddenly. In truth they are his response to much prayer. Can you sleep without one lock?'

"For a month I had no lock on the side door to the yard. I believed I would die, but I prayed that God would let me ascend to heaven after purgatory, where I would do penance for the other locks. I went back to work at the shoe-factory; I slept, though not well. One day the father at the hospital told me: 'Take the lock off the back door, my son.' Now he was certainly consigning me to death, but I obeyed him. It was only important to me now that I die with the name of Christ on my lips. When the father at last told me to take the third lock off, too, the one on the front door, he said: 'You will indeed die someday, as we all will. Do you see that it doesn't matter when you die, but instead whether your soul is true while you live?'

"I took off the third lock and prayed harder. One early morning I woke up very suddenly. Someone was in the room with me. Though it was light, I did not dare open my eyes. I prayed fervently, and gave my soul to God. The person in my room hit me and said something which seemed to be in a language I didn't understand. As I waited to die, this thought struck me like a thunderbolt: I am happy. I had never been happy before, and the feeling astonished me. I prayed and prayed and I forgot about the intruder in the room, until she pulled at the covers and I opened my eyes. It was my sister's two-year-old child trying to climb onto my bed.

"Why should I die like I was, a frightened and miserable mental patient, when it would be happiness to die close to God and prepared for heaven? I said to the father at the hospital that I would spend whatever time I had left praying and purifying my soul. I told him that I wanted nothing else. He cautioned me to practice moderation. But he brought me to a Carmelite father. As soon as I met that monk, who owned nothing and thought of nothing but God, I knew that I had found what I wanted for myself. In six months I had taken the vows."

The brother's story made me nervous. I'd seen soon enough that here was a prime case of a stunt if there ever was one. The Swede had changed himself into someone else as completely as poor Cinderella had. It was so much of a stunt that I began to get suspicious that the monsignor, Father Jeremy, had set this ride up for me just so that I would see the legitimate ways of changing myself that the Church had in store for me, if I wanted to get hooked. I told myself I wasn't one bit interested in getting hooked. It was one thing to find out if there might be a religious explanation for the energy: it was another thing to worry about God and Jesus and your soul all your life. To me that was just a lot of rigamarole, and I wasn't going to clutter up the energy with any rigamarole. I was just going to see Father Jeremy to get some information.

I couldn't see the reason for praying, for one thing. And all these vows that the Swedish brother had taken, the chastity and so forth: I didn't like the sound of it. I thought he was obviously forcing the changes; he was just mounting the locks now on himself. "How does this work, though, Brother?" I asked him, "If you don't mind my asking? Don't you get the urge sometimes to lock up your cell at the monastery, for example?"

He laughed again. "Sure, I am sometimes afraid. I think perhaps another brother will take my cross. I thought you would cost me something by riding with me today. Suddenly I was thinking the car and the toll-money belonged to me. It is hard to be at my old home, where all the insanities happened. But even at the monastery I can forget that everything I have, including my life, belongs to God. But the vows remind me. They tell me who I have promised myself to be. When I think of them, then I am no longer afraid. Anyone can come in and take anything they wish, take it all, take my life, because how can they take what is already God's? My vows are my friends. They have set me free."

We left the Taconic Parkway and drove northeast into the Berkshire hills, low and round and deep blue-purple in the late afternoon, with a yellow sprinkling of the last of the birch-leaves on the bare trees. The fields were still green — it was the beginning of November; on both sides of the road, black and white dairy-cows sat munching on the grass near red barns with round-topped silos. Signs saying 'Apple Cider' with dried paint dripping from the letters leaned against the mailboxes. White wooden farmhouses stood right against the highway, with brick chimneys running up their sides. Narrow roads wound off up into the hills. To me it was a story-book, a picture from a magazine. It never would have crossed my mind that such places existed outside of cigarette advertisements or the drawings in your elementary-school reader. "How long does this go on, Brother Stephen?"

"What? Does what go on?"

"These places. These farms."

"Yes, I do not know. Massachusetts, Vermont, New Hampshire, part of Maine also. All very nice. I have been. Nicer than Hackensack."

"So what about the rest of Maine?"

"What? There are forests."

I wanted to pump him about all the places he knew, but he didn't want to talk. I watched him there, bent over the wheel with his lips moving slightly and his brown robe flopping over the gearshift, crawling along at thirty miles an hour through the hills. On the upgrades he wouldn't bother to shift down, so the transmission rattled and groaned. He never noticed. He was getting ready to begin his life again. As we crossed the hills toward his monastery, I thought I could feel the tension in him seep out the windows and dissolve among the farms. Suddenly I thought: What makes me decide his vows are so extreme? How do I know what goes on in his monastery? or what goes on in that farmhouse there, where someone's just turning on a lamp against the evening? or what goes on up that side-road there, or in Massachusetts, Vermont, New Hampshire, Maine, in any of the states I've never been to? I've been complaining to Margherita about our friends, I thought, how they can't accept what's happening to me because they don't know anywhere but Jersey, and they don't understand what different kinds of people there are — they think everybody who isn't like themselves is either crazy or bad news

56

or else not completely human; yet hadn't I had the same feelings in myself? But here, look: on the map on the seat in the dim light, all those roads scribbling out like twigs over the page; and outside, the miles, the hills, the entire world turning over towards the night: couldn't Margherita and Vin and I find our own place, too, where we could change, the same as Brother Stephen had found his?

He bumped us over a driveway and stopped the car by stalling it. Up ahead in the dark was a lit doorway in a three-story building shaped like a barn; faint glimmers of light showed in rows of small windows. Other dim buildings sailed on the outskirts in the night. "That way," Brother Stephen said, pointing to the lit doorway, and he disappeared. I went to the doorway and opened it. An old brother who'd lost most of his teeth stood up suddenly in the hall, startling me. "Come." He led me down a corridor lit by a single bulb to a small room with a cot in it. "Mass is said in the chapel at midnight and at six and eight in the morning. You are welcome here. Good night." He was gone before I opened my mouth to ask where Father Jeremy was and furthermore when and where dinner was. There wasn't a sound in the building or outside in the night. It didn't seem like a good start to knock on someone's door or shout down the corridor. I reminded myself that there were other places than Jersey, and that I was certainly in one of those places. During the night I dreamed of monks chanting.

A white mist filled the morning. The air was clear for only the first four feet above the ground, so that I could see the red monastery buildings only up to their windows. The buildings stood around a duck-pond; a stream spread out into it quietly. Above the water, and down from the cloudy undersurface of the mist, drops of sparkling condensation hung like strings of beads in the light. I wandered around the place, trying to figure out where everybody was, with my hungry stomach growling in the silence. Suddenly the chanting I'd heard in my sleep burst out of the mist.

The chapel was right there, with its steeple faint and seeming distant above in the white. The clean sound of the chanting drew me inside. They were celebrating the High Mass. The chanters stood on the far side of the altar, behind a heavy ironwork screen, and through it I could make out sections of their robes and patches of their faces and held-up hands. Mumble, mumble, the congregation of a dozen other monks and some local people said some of the ritual, and then again, without any warning, the chanters' voices leapt out at full strength and rolled through that stuffy little building like a charge of blasting-gel set off in the air. It was sung all in unison, so that it sounded infinitely deep, but without an interior; that music seemed to me as cool and clear as the energy itself, as if they had tried to represent it in sound. After each chant, I thought I sensed a feeling of rest in the chapel; I thought each blast of music must be loosening another layer of tension in the monks' minds. For a moment, nobody in the chapel had anything against anyone; I would have sworn to it. As I thought this, the mass was over. From behind the screen the chanting fathers filed out in a single line down the center aisle. The energy began silently buzzing under my scalp as they passed me, which took me by surprise, since I hadn't been trying to concentrate. I started wondering just what was going on in this place. The fathers filed out the door, and the energy faded.

I waited in the chapel near the door, in case Father Jeremy might come in; I hadn't noticed him there at the mass, but I thought maybe he might have noticed me. For a while I idly stared at a fat little lady kneeling straight as a ramrod on a prayer-stool in a side-chapel and offering up Hail Mary's to the Virgin. I'd noticed the woman before; she'd limped forward to receive the host during the mass with the help of a cane, as if she had a bad case of arthritis. Her cane rested now against a pew. Kneeling there with no coughing, no shuffling, not one bit of shifting to ease the joints, without moving anything but her lips, she prayed for what must have been twenty minutes. She probably forgets

58

she's the fat little lady with arthritis while she's down there muttering, I said to myself; no wonder she goes at it. Prayer could be a kind of stunt for her; it's obvious, once you think of it. If she concentrates hard enough on prayer or anything else, she's going to forget her pains; haven't I stopped feeling the bottom half of my body now and then when the energy was pouring out? Maybe this fat lady is burning with the energy right now, while I'm watching her.

In a flash I was down on the prayer-stool next to her, muttering Hail Mary's to myself. I didn't believe in the Virgin, but, I thought, so what? I concentrated my mind on the words of the prayer, which no one forgets after a Catholic childhood, and I tried to keep the other thoughts out. Soon enough, the energy was piling up in my shoulders and pouring down the backs of my arms and streaming outward through my held-up hands. At that moment, the monastery made sense to me. It was a place where people got together to do the God-stunt. Vows, penance, austerity, prayers, all of it: it was the monks' grand stunt to get free of the ordinary distractions of life so that they could concentrate their minds and rev up their energies. They did it all day; they spent their lives at it. They probably have so much energy going, I thought, that they broadcast it: I'll bet I picked it up when they filed out of the church after the mass. Some of them probably radiated from every pore, all day long. The idea dazzled me.

I started thinking of all those phrases that the nuns had drilled into me when I was a kid: "Jesus is the light of the world" — "God's radiance" — "Saint So-and-So was burning with the fire of the Holy Spirit" — Of course I naturally assumed that this was just a way of speaking. But it wasn't. This was a real light they were talking about; it was a real burning. They told you that plain enough, but for some reason they never let on that it was something everyone could feel with a little concentration-effort. Instead, they harped on God and heaven and hell and all the rest of the rigamarole. And meanwhile they stunted their lives away.

Wait till I tell Margherita that my so-called crazy ideas are the secret rites of the one holy Catholic and apostolic Church! My head was spinning with it. I barrelled out of the chapel to look for Father Jeremy. The old brother who kept the door to the main building said that the father sent his welcome and would see me in an hour.

I waited on the footbridge over the stream, watching the ducks upend themselves to feed in the pond. Their black-and-white tails twitched and pointed to the sky. Everything was bright; the sun shone. For the first time, I could see that the monastery lay in a narrow valley between the hills. A fire-tower stood on a summit in the distance. As I thought for a while, I decided that maybe it was right for the monks to concentrate their minds secretly, and to talk to people just about God and hell; if they talked about the energy, who would believe them? Everybody would think they were crazy. They had to make the thing approachable for people. They made up the God part and the Holy Spirit and the rest, so that people would pray and learn to concentrate their minds on the prayers. Anyone who worked hard enough at it would soon enough discover the energy for himself. He'd go to a priest and say, 'Listen, Father, what is this?' And the priest would answer: 'Now you understand.'

It made perfect sense. But I could see there was no way I could call up Margherita long-distance and tell her that I wasn't alone after all. She'd think I'd have cracked for sure. I'd probably have to tell her that I was converted to the Church. It would give me a cover for hanging around the monastery to learn about the energy and all the rules about concentrating.

Plans to move us up to the Berkshires, not too far from Father Jeremy, began running through my head at top speed. The night before, Brother Stephen had driven us through a small city nearby called Pittsfield: I could look for a job there. We'd rent our house in West New York for the winter. Margherita wouldn't have to work. We'd make new friends. We'd get on to our feet again.

Father Jeremy was standing there next to me, resting his arms on the railing of the bridge. He startled me; his soft handsome looks were gone. He'd lost a lot of weight, and the skin was tight around the tendons of his neck. Instead of contact lenses, he wore large octagonal gold-rimmed glasses which half-hid his thick eyebrows and which made him look studious. In place of his trim clerical suit were the robes. The good humor was still in his eyes. "How's West New York faring?" he asked me.

"Faring? Oh, it's okay. Listen, Father, I wanted to ask you — well, first of all, thank you for letting me come up here."

"How could I resist after such a tantalizing letter?" he said. "I'm glad you came."

"Yeah, well thanks." I couldn't wait for any more of the formalities. "Listen, Father" —

"I'm all ears."

"Okay now this isn't exactly what I came up here to ask you, but" — I didn't know if there was a proper way to let it be known that you'd discovered the energy. I decided I should be asking for instruction. "Look, you know when they talk about the light of Christ and the radiance of God and so on? Now is this a real light, Father?"

"I never would have guessed that was it," Father Jeremy said, looking at me with an amused expression in his eyes. He thought a minute. "Is God's radiance real. Do you mean is God real?"

"No, we'll get to that, maybe, but I just mean is this light something you can see? Can you feel this radiance radiating? When they talk about it, what are they talking about, see what I mean?"

"These are things I don't know much about," Father Jeremy said. "It is God's nature to be radiant, and it is said that when a soul ascends to heaven it is dazzled by that radiance. — I can see this isn't what you're after."

I'd been shaking my head. "This is the kind of story the Church tells, sure; I know that. But what I'm trying to say is" — I supposed they had to keep pretty guarded about the truth of the thing. You couldn't just spring it on people, as I already knew well enough. I'd have to come out and tell him. "See, I stumbled on it myself, Father — the energy and the radiance. It wasn't through praying, though, it was by doing the stunts, like the one we did on you? I just concentrated on the stunts the way the little lady with arthritis in your congregation here concentrates on her Hail Mary's, and watch out, there it was."

He was looking at me very puzzled, but smiling. "I've lost you now, Joey, Let's back up a bit. You were talking about"—

"Come on, Father; I was talking about what goes on in this monastery. You and the other fathers and the lady with arthritis, you're all just using the praying and the chanting and the rigamarole to concentrate your minds so you can build up the energy. I told you, I already figured it out, so there isn't any point in holding back on me. You don't have to worry about my springing it on people, because nobody back home is the slightest bit interested. And I need to know, so I can stop making mistakes."

He was frowning at his hands, and he said with a bit of annoyance in his voice: "Give me the benefit of the doubt and tell me what you're talking about, will you?"

What was this, their initiation test? I thought: Who knows? Maybe they have to do it this way. "All right," I told him. "Everybody here prays, right? They concentrate their minds, and their energy starts to pile up, because that's what happens when you concentrate your mind. The lady with arthritis does it with her Hail Mary's; you and the other fathers, you do it with your chanting; Brother Stephen does it with his vow not to own anything; and I did it with my stunts. If you concentrate hard enough and you pile up enough energy, then the energy radiates from your skin. Isn't this what the Church calls God's radiance? If you radiate enough of it, for all I know it'll become visible, although I haven't seen it; maybe this is what the Church calls God's light? Isn't that what all you fathers are doing up here, building up your own lights and just calling it God's light so as to make it approachable for people?"

Father Jeremy was blinking his eyes and leaning over the railing of the bridge, staring at the reflections of the sun that glittered in the water.

"See what I mean, Father?" I asked him. "Look, you saw me yourself, the first time I caught on. It was the day we stole your limousine? The cops had finally stopped us, and you came walking up. Just then, the energy was all around, and I didn't know what was happening. I always thought you saw me and understood."

He murmured: "I thought I did, too. I thought you were on drugs, Joey." He looked at me sharply. "I'm sorry. Perhaps that wasn't it at all?"

I laughed at him. "Come on, Father, quit playing around, will you?" But he shook his head, smiling slightly, and said nothing. The thought struck me that he didn't know about the energy. But I didn't believe it. He was deciding how to deal with my unorthodox approach to the energy and with my using a non-religious kind of concentration: that must be it.

In a minute he said: "I'm trying to place what you've told me, Joey. It's definitely true that people can have unusual sensations when they pray. I myself can feel very clean afterwards inside, as if I'd been swept out: unquestionably a physiological feeling, a real feeling in the body. One hears or reads also of the devout experiencing light, or radiance, or the presence of God. I take it you're speaking along these lines?"

"Okay," I said, "probably I am. Except I'm not devout; excuse me, Father, but I don't even go to church, and I don't see what this whole thing has to do with God at all. Why does it have to be God's radiance? Can't you just work at the radiance in yourself? Isn't that what you do, Father?"

"No." He tapped his palm rapidly for emphasis. "Prayer may be pleasant and bring pleasant sensations, but that is not a reason to pray. To make prayer into a kind of pleasure is a bad mistake which devout people can make, and it's a mistake for just the reason you admit to: this pleasure shuts out God. True prayer seeks to reach God. True prayer asks forgiveness, and it purifies the soul."

I was getting pretty impatient with him. "That all sounds real nice, Father, and I don't mean to be disrespectful, but everything you say assumes there is a God, it just assumes it, see? because what if there isn't one? If the praying and the chanting and all the rest are to purify the soul like you say, then why do you want to put God in there to muddle up the purity? The energy is empty. When you concentrate your mind and the energy builds up, then soon everything is filled with it, so there isn't any room for any disturbances, and everything is peaceful and pure and still; but the energy itself is empty. This is just what makes it pure. It doesn't have anything inside it. So how can there be a God in there? and a Christ and saints and angels playing harps? How can there be a soul in there? That crowd of ideas you fathers pray to, it just seems like a lot of confusion to me, not any peacefulness and purity."

He'd been waiting to get a word in, and I was afraid I'd completely offended him; but in fact I'd finally got him interested. "I haven't experienced this kind of thing, so I don't know how to evaluate it," he said, turning towards me and tapping his palm again, "but the point of prayer, the point of penance — one might even say the point of religion is to forget oneself; is for you and me to abandon ourselves so God may live inside us in our place"—

I interrupted him: "Sure, okay, change yourself, just completely lose yourself in the energy, I've sometimes thought about this, but what I don't see is why you keep talking about God."

"It's what I'm trying to tell you. Say that you have emptied yourself of yourself, of your desires and of your fears, and you have accepted God within you as Jesus Christ our savior instructs us — only to discover that God is empty, or worse, that there is no God after all, but only the void — this seems to me a deeply frightening idea. Isn't it? Don't you find it so? I mean, what would one have, then?"

I had come up here to ask him, but he was asking me; and what did I know? I was crestfallen. "The emptiness is full, though, Father; it's full of energy and stillness. Your mind fills with it and fills with it. You don't need any God in there. Because I know what you're talking about: you're talking about something else, when your thoughts empty out and there isn't any energy in its place, there's just darkness. You just become less and less, and that is frightening, believe me. I thought I was going to die when it happened to me. This is what I originally came up to ask you, how to keep clear of the bad times."

But I could see that he didn't know. He didn't know anything about the energy and the stillness, or about the darkness, either; he didn't know anything I'd wanted him to know. The things we'd been talking about were nothing but ideas to him.

"The light, full emptiness and the dark, empty emptiness." He was nodding quickly. It intrigued him. I had the feeling that once he put something into the category of an intellectual idea, he could toss it up and down and around no matter what it referred to. But I think he saw how disappointed I was, and he let it drop. "I can tell you one thing, Joey. If you have faith, and if you hold to that faith, no emptiness can harm you. I think God has been seeking you, for he seeks all of us, and I believe you have been turning away from him."

"I'm not turning toward him or away from him. I just don't feel him in there" — At my raised voice, the ducks burst up from under the bridge and flew down the pond, trailing their hanging feet on the water, until they settled again among some weeds that grew along the shore. "I just want to understand what I feel, Father. I want to know who I am and what I'm supposed to do. It doesn't do any good to call the thing that's changing me and pushing me 'God.' It's just a name, and it doesn't mean anything to me."

"Don't just look for yourself, Joey. If you look only for yourself and don't look for God, you will never reach your goal."

"Is this what you're doing, Father? Is this why you became a Carmelite, to look for God?"

"Yes. And for peace." He added after a minute: "I kept stumbling when I looked for myself."

"I guess I've got something to apologize about there — embarrassing you like that in front of people."

"Oh, no. Don't think about it." He looked at the glittering water. "It's true, though, the world seemed such fun there, for a while. I almost quit." I think he meant the priesthood; but he didn't say. "I am glad I did not."

"And you're really convinced about God and heaven and the whole thing, Father? This isn't just a way you fathers talk so as to explain it to people?"

"No, how can you say that? Life is so complicated, even here; why should we want to make it more complicated? Do you really believe such a thing?"

"No. I did, I guess."

Bells rang from the steeple. "Lunchtime," Father Jeremy said. "Will you eat? Will you stay a while? We'll talk again?"

"I'm hungry; thank you, Father." We tramped across the footbridge towards the refectory. From the weeds, the ducks came out quacking, and they swam into the middle of the pond.

FOUR

I LEFT THE monastery that afternoon. I told myself that what I ought to do is hitchhike back home and admit to Margherita that Father Jeremy didn't have any answers for me. What would I do after that, though? Settle down again to live like a hermit in my own house, hiding from my neighbors and going to some high-priced doctor who wanted me to be happy with canasta again?

I walked up the side-road out of the narrow valley of the monastery and onto the state highway which ran along the ridge. As I looked north and east, where new ridge after new ridge followed one another into the distance, with a quiet farm resting nearby on the downward slope and another climbing the up-slope beyond — as I looked at this, I couldn't see myself going back to West New York, to all that consternation and those nosey people, for even one day. There was nothing I wanted there, except for Margherita and Vin. I wanted to go on; I wanted to explore all the places that the Swedish brother, Brother Stephen, had told me he had seen. It didn't matter that Father Jeremy didn't have any explanation for me. If he had, then I would have just had to exchange the fuss of West New York for the fuss of the Church. Instead I was alone, and I was glad. Something was going to happen; I was going to change, as much as Brother Stephen had, maybe, but in some different way, in a way that would be my own.

When I'd left West New York, I'd told Margherita that I'd be away probably three or four days, since I'd thought there'd be a lot to discuss with Father Jeremy. But I'd only been away a bit more than twenty-four hours. There was some time left to look around. I was still thinking in terms of the plan I'd had about the monastery: I wanted to find a quiet town with a job where we could spend just a few months to begin with, and we'd rent out our house in West New York, so as not to jump too far too fast, but to see how it worked being away. I thought Margherita might accept this. She wouldn't have to work, and in a strange town there wouldn't be anyone we would have to explain things to. I got out my road-map of New England and sat on a stone wall covered with ivy, with the red leaves curling up and drying with the fall. Vermont was only fifteen miles north up the road, New Hampshire another forty miles east; east across New Hampshire was Maine. These were the states Brother Stephen had mentioned in the car the night before. Here and there on the map were small cities, maybe with factories in them and a job: Manchester, Concord, Portland, Bangor. I stuck out my thumb at the northbound cars.

Farmers stopped for me in their pickup-trucks. I stared out the windows as they drove. In Vermont, the hills grew steeper and the farmhouses changed: large and square and plain, white with green roofs, each one connected by a covered passageway to a barn just as plain. A farmer about sixty who wheezed heavily through his nose and took me into New Hampshire said the covered passageways let you get to the barn when the snow was in. Volkswagens passed us heading north with skis strapped to their backs. Near the towns, the highways were cluttered with motels, and along the main streets, large white houses with green shutters stood back behind clean lawns. It didn't look like there'd be jobs in such places. We reached Manchester: this was what I needed. Five miles outside the city, there was countryside where we could live, but in town the river was lined with old red brick factories, each with a little steeple and with the name of the company painted across the face. The farmer who was driving me dropped me downtown at the state employment office just before it closed. But they didn't have anything I could use: just short-order cooks and clerk-typists. "Business is slow," the crewcut in there said.

I stayed the night in the YMCA in Concord, fifteen miles north, and tried for jobs there in the morning. There was nothing. I tried Portsmouth, New Hampshire; in the afternoon I hitched to Portland, Maine, and looked there. "You could try the paper-mills," the young woman in the state employment office in Portland said. She had a bleached white streak in her hair. "The mills start having some turnover about now, with the winter coming," she said. I asked her where the paper-mills were. She looked at me like I should be pitied, but like she herself didn't have the time for that. "Up north," she said. "Try our Bangor office. Will you tell them we directed you? We need that for our files."

It was my third night out; I had to call Margherita. I didn't want to talk to her, though, until I'd found something that possibly looked right, presuming I could find anything; it didn't seem as easy as I thought. I sent her a telegram, which made me feel that what I was doing was very important, since I'd never sent a telegram before. "I'm looking around a bit," it said. "Will call in a couple days. Squeeze Vin for me. And you." The plump woman in the Western Union office embarrassed me by counting the words and reading them back to me.

In a '51 Studebaker, a kid with a forest of hair and a ready lecture on the Bible drove me into Bangor that night. I remember being struck by the quiet of the place. Nothing was open on the main street but three bars. In front of them, pickup-trucks smelling of cows were parked on the diagonal. It was cold; a half-inch of snow lay beside the railroad tracks that ran through the town. I stayed in a brick hotel above one of the bars and lay awake with the noise of voices below. There was a telephone book on the night-table. I didn't see any paper-mills listed in it. I almost called Margherita, but I finally decided I would give myself one more day.

"Loader? Can you work a loader? Don't mind working outside, do you?" the old man in the employment office asked me in the morning. I said I could work a loader inside or outside. "Gets mighty cold up there, though," he said, nodding with a grin, seeming to enjoy the idea of me freezing to death while he spent the winter in the tropics of Bangor. "Up there" was Millinocket, seventy miles farther north. There were two big paper-mills there. I walked back out to the highway, trying to feel confident about what I was doing.

A very fat greeting-card salesman in a grey suit stopped for me in his Plymouth Barracuda. As we drove north, the country changed again. On the ridges, the purple of the bare trees was mixed now with the green of spruce and pine, and the farms were fewer and smaller and weatherbeaten, with junk cars lying in the front yards. Then the farms dropped behind altogether, and the trees moved down close against the road. From one high point, I looked west and north across the ridges for what must have been fifty miles, and the trees grew over it all, without a house, without a road to be seen, though the sunlight glinted here and there in the distance on a lost pond. The Maine Woods had begun. The salesman who was driving me — he spent most of the trip describing a scheme he had to corner the pencil-sharpener market — said the woods kept right on going into Canada with hardly a break, and then better than a thousand miles farther, through to the Arctic. Since I couldn't believe a man of his size would go anywhere near such a strenuous place as the Arctic, I figured he didn't actually know about the woods and had exaggerated them a good deal for effect. Afterwards I found out that he hadn't.

As the road cut through the forest, with the edge of the trees close in on either side, I could see far in among the criss-cross maze of dead lower branches, till they matted together in a black dark. I asked the salesman if people ever went in there.

"Loggers, hunters, oh, sure," he said. "Have a breakdown, freeze, get lost, go nuts, happens every winter. They go in, they don't come out." He chuckled a bit, apparently feeling very satisfied about it all.

After more than an hour, the trees suddenly halted, and we were driving down a green open slope patched with snow. Ahead at the bottom of the clearing, a black river, the Penobscot, crossed beneath the highway, and beside it stood one of those long old red brick factories: the East Millinocket mill. Beyond it two miles up the slope, the woods began again. We turned west along the river. The salesman told me that until a few years before, they used to float the logs down the river out of the forest to the mill. "They use trucks now," he said. "Less labor." Soon above us, on the slope, the green steel of the new Millinocket mill stood gleaming with a thousand windows. "I'll show you where I stay when I'm here," the salesman said. "The widow likes an introduction." And he drove me down the main street of Millinocket, past the brick commercial buildings and onto a side street of small white houses. "ROOMS," a sign said in a window.

"Mrs. Rose," the salesman announced, "this young fellow may want bed and board on a weekly basis, if the mill takes him." Mrs. Rose was a tall old lady with white hair in a hair-net and a flower-print dress and a grey shawl on her shoulders. We stood in the hall and she looked me over suspiciously. "He pays in advance," she said.

Mrs. Rose's house was as close with itself as she was with her money, and a good deal older, with low ceilings and low doorways and small windows that had tiny panes with circular flaws in them. On the doors were black iron latches that you had to lift to open, and the living room was cluttered with high-backed furniture, with claws at the ends of the wooden arms, and with lace towels draped over the backs of the chairs where your head went. "I'll drive you to the mill," the salesman said; he held up a fat finger: "Opportunities! Opportunities!" probably thinking of his pencil-sharpeners. It was the oddballs and loners like him who were to help me out on the road. They understood long before I did that I was one of them.

As the salesman drove me up the ridge towards the mill, I could see below us the white houses of Millinocket packed together along the river in the middle of a clearing. The woods climbed down the ridges from every direction and closed close around the clearing, not two miles out from the Protestant church that stood in a little lawn in the center of the town. It seemed like the clearing protected the houses and the people from the danger of the woods, but the woods protected all of Millinocket from the danger of the world.

They hired me at the mill. The job was to unload logs from the backs of the logging-trucks, using a big pair of machine-tongs mounted on a loader that wasn't much different from my hilo back home. You swung the logs end-on four at a time into the stripping-saw, which ripped off the bark and then sent the logs naked into the mill. I watched the supervisor run the loader for a while — the man I was replacing had quit — and then I walked back down into town, feeling scared. I knew I couldn't be positive that I hadn't somehow gone off the deep end without realizing it. There was no one to consult with. I went into a phone-booth to call Margherita, but I hung up after one ring at our house. When it came down to it, I knew I wasn't sure enough of what I was doing to be able to stand up to talking to her. She'd get nervous and worried and start quizzing me about what in God's name was I doing up there and why hadn't I come home to Jersey and was I sure I was all right? I didn't want to get angry with her; and I didn't want her to get the upper hand, either, and persuade me to come home. I still wanted to take the chance that I might find something if I stayed away. I spent some time in the phone-booth complaining to myself how stubborn she was. I told myself that I shouldn't have to persuade her, that she ought to already be up here feeling excited about the new town and looking for a place to live, instead of everything being uphill for me. Even as I thought this, I knew I was lying and that I had no right not to phone her. But it seemed like too much of a risk, and I couldn't find the courage. Finally I sent her another telegram to tell her I was resting in a very decent place and not to worry.

The electric sign on the Great Northern Federal Savings building said nine degrees above zero when I walked up the slope to the paper-mill in the morning. All I had was a jacket and scarf, and my fingers were red and numb by the time I punched in. The supervisor on the loading-dock, whose name was Gordon, thought I was joking when I told him it was the coldest weather I'd ever been in. He said maybe I ought to get a bit used to it, since it got down to twenty-five, thirty below there in January and February. At first I thought it was him that was joking; then I decided Millinocket was obviously out of the question as a place to live, since Margherita wouldn't be able to stand it, and if she could, I couldn't. But after a couple of days of working in the cold, I changed my opinion about it. It seemed to quiet my mind. Like a blowtorch, but smelling of the clean sawdust of pines, the freezing air cut into my head with every breath I took and burned out my worrying thoughts. The whine of the stripping-saw and the endless growl of the logging-trucks as they backed and filed were blended together in my ears into a roaring silence.

I tried to concentrate my mind on moving the logs, and the energy stoked up inside me and burned on my skin and kept my hands and feet warm. Far off into the bright air, into the woods beyond the river-valley, dark lakes sparkled in the sun. I wanted to make my mind as still as that distant water. It seemed to me it would be possible in Millinocket. I thought it would just be the work of a few weeks, if I concentrated hard enough and gave my agitations to the cold. Gordon, the dock supervisor, told me he'd been offered a transfer to a job inside the mill a couple years back, and he'd turned it down. I thought I understood.

Gordon became friendly when he caught on that I knew about cars. He himself was a fanatic about Volkswagens. He invited me over to see his junkyard. "I got a new '57," he told me. "Good year." He never said more than ten or fifteen words at one time. His back yard and barn were a horticultural nursery of Volkswagens in various stages of budding and grafting and flowering. He had all the parts perfectly organized down to the last machine-screw, and there wasn't a spot of grease out of place anywhere. He was a little grey-haired guy about forty who kept his lips pursed all the time, and indoors and out he wore a grey fisherman's hat with little round holes in it. He kept taking it off and scratching his head and putting it back on again. His wife, Joyce, who was blond and slow and bigger than him, didn't like to talk much more than he did, and when they did say something, at first I had to ask them "What?" half the time, because their Maine accent was so strange to me. They never raised their voices. It seemed like the years of cold had frozen their lives to the essentials, as if they'd stashed their feelings a long time back in some deep protected cellar and had mostly forgotten them. I worked the entire weekend on his '57 Volkswagen — later, after we'd rebuilt it, he gave it to me for seventy-five dollars — and not once did he or his wife ever ask my why I'd left Jersey, and did the ring I wore mean I had a wife and maybe kids, and did I go to church or play cards or watch football, and what did I think about politics. I probably could have lived in Millinocket ten years without anybody asking me for an explanation of why I was there.

Each morning when the logging trucks woke up the town by roaring into the woods, I felt surer that I had found the place I wanted. The people were decent and wouldn't bother us; the pay was good and the housing cheap; Margherita could swim in the summer and Vin could go sledding in the winter: what more could we ask? Next to this peaceful Yankee clearing, West New York seemed like a jungle. But the more days that passed and the more Millinocket made sense to me, the more I was afraid to go down to that phone-booth and call Margherita. I kept debating with her in my mind, telling her not to be stubborn and to give my idea a chance, but I always kept losing the argument. I couldn't think up the right way to persuade her. I knew she would see Millinocket as a kind of exile. I couldn't delay much longer, since she was probably already thinking I'd gone crazy again; but that only made it harder to call her. I kept sending off telegrams with a sentence or two, knowing it was wrong and hating myself, but not being able to see my way around it. I began to get nervous, the way I had before when my mind was ready to go wrong on me. One afternoon, after I'd been on the job about a week, I pulled the wrong lever on the loader and dropped some logs on the dock a couple feet from where Gordon was standing. He didn't say a thing; he turned his back on me when I apologized.

That night I went down to Bangor with a couple of the log-ging-truck drivers to see a Western movie. I was about ready to give in and go home, and I didn't want to have to think about it. After the movie on the way back to Millinocket, as I slept sitting up in the back of the car, I dreamed I was sitting in the lobby of a big old wooden hotel, the kind there'd been in the movie. I seemed to know it was in California, in the eighteen-eighties or nineties. It wasn't myself sitting there exactly, but somebody else who was myself, the way it can happen in dreams. Couples kept going on past me and into the upstairs — this was the kind of place it was, but with a very respectable air about it, considering that it was the frontier. I was waiting, but I couldn't remember for what or for whom. Finally a woman I'd seen walking around in a fancy long red low-cut dress, the kind the bar-hostesses wear in television westerns, came over to where I was sitting and said I should go on upstairs. She mentioned the name of a woman, but I didn't hear it well. I went on up a big curving staircase with a bannister painted gold and down a long corridor with red plush walls. I could hear laughter in the rooms behind the doors. Then on one door I saw the number 516, and there was a rush of feeling in my throat and eyes, half of pain and half delight. Without opening the door, I was in the room. A woman with her back to me was standing at the edge of a modern shower-stall, rinsing out a pair of khaki pants in the shower. She'd been in the water herself, and her hair was up in a towel. Her bare skin dripped and shone. She turned around, and we embraced with an emotion that burst up from under my stomach and flooded my mind so that I forgot what I was seeing; it was a more powerful desire than I'd ever let myself feel when I was awake. As she unwound the towel from her hair, which was black and straight, I noticed she was an Oriental woman. Then I remembered that this was what kept us from being together. Just then the dream changed.

I was standing in what they call a pavilion, a sort of veranda standing free without a house, a bit like the one they had in Millinocket in the town park. In the dream it was built into the side of a hill, and across a small canyon, two hundred feet from where I stood, a waterfall shot down a wall of rock and churned up a circle of white water in a dark pool below. Beside the waterfall, vines with enormous green leaves hung down the rock wall. A woman stood facing the fall, rinsing her clothes in the pool. I saw myself then: dressed in heavy embroidered robes, I was watching the woman from above, half-hidden in the shadow of the pavilion. Her bare back was turned to me; below her waist she was hidden in the white water. Suddenly she stopped her washing and walked up under the waterfall so the stream of it blasted down on her upturned forehead, and she shook herself and whirled her arms so the clothes in her hands whipped around like flags. My throat tightened with longing to call out her name, but I knew that if she saw me there she would be very angry. I thought I would give up my life to see her full form without her knowing.

Suddenly there was a splash below me, and, naked himself, a man was bounding out into the water. I recognized him; I was amazed that he was her lover; I was stunned that she would have a lover. He paddled toward her, yelling happily a nickname which I didn't know she used. I was sure that in a moment she would turn around to him and that I would see her form at last. I knew she would also see me spying on them. But I couldn't force myself to turn away.

Again the dream changed. It was just one picture. I was standing in a dusty street, knocking on a rough wooden door in a long wall made of mud and straw. I was young: fifteen, maybe. I knocked, and from behind the wall came the sound of splashing water and a girl's laughter. I banged on the door with both fists. There was no answer except for more laughter. I wanted to scream at her for mocking me. I woke up. We were in Millinocket. The other men were riding me for talking in my sleep.

The longing I'd felt in the dream was still pressuring up in my throat in the morning, and it stayed for days afterward. Suddenly I was looking at women again. Everything was suddenly changed in my mind. I didn't want the energy of concentration any more, except to free more of the energy I felt now, the energy of desire. I couldn't stop myself from walking down to the high school at lunch-hour and staring. The glimpse of a girl's walk or the angle of a face would remind me of the women in the dream, and desire would rush through me like a hot breath. The flesh on these bodies that used to seem sweaty and shameful to me, the way Catholics learn it, seemed as precious to me now as the Oriental woman in the hotel and as infinitely clean as the waterfall under the pavilion. In my bed I imagined Margherita under my hands and felt panicked that maybe I was doomed to do nothing else but imagine her for the rest of my life, because calling home or even sending a telegram was impossible now. I was sure Margherita would be able to tell how agitated I was, and I knew I'd say something to make her nervous, and then she'd never come. But I had to stay in Millinocket: it seemed the more days I lived there, the more of a total defeat it would be to admit that I had to go home. Sometimes I'd even think that Margherita would be better off without me, so maybe it would be all right for me to go after other women. Then I'd think of Vin or of how many times Margherita had helped me out, and I'd be even more ashamed.

Three days after I'd had the dream, I spent an afternoon in Gordon's yard, putting the finishing touches on the '57 Volkswagen. I put solvent on some tar-spots on the fenders. As I picked up the hose to wash the fenders down, some high-school girls out on the sidewalk let out a glad shriek, the way they do when the boys come up behind them. Right then, a memory from when I first knew Margherita, a moment I'd completely forgotten, splashed up into my mind. After I'd first met her and had taken her out to see a couple of baseball games, without drumming up much interest on either side, one Sunday I decided on impulse to walk over to her house, having nothing else in particular to do that day. No one answered the door, but just in case she might be out back, I went up the the side-alley to the yard behind the house. There was Margherita, dressed in shorts and a man's shirt too big for herself, putting water on her father's flower-beds with the garden hose. This is why she hadn't heard me at the door. She caught sight of me: zip, she trained the hose on me. Of course I closed.in and wrestled with her for the nozzle, and soon enough we were both soaked.

Shriek! went Margherita, when she noticed how wet she was — it was the high-school girls' shriek in Millinocket that called up the memory — Margherita ran to the back steps of her house to go inside to change her clothes. But in order to open the back door, she was forced to turn towards me a second, and since her soaked shirt clung to her skin, I could see through the cloth to her shape as she turned, as well as any young man could ask. It was this that I had forgotten. She was slim then, and her hair was short and straight to her shoulders, instead of the bubble-cut she'd had done soon afterwards. I'd forgotten that; I'd forgotten her as I'd first desired her, just as I'd forgotten everything else in that clear memory, the red wooden steps which had long since been ripped out for concrete, an out-of-date radio-aerial strapped to the drain-pipe and looking like a helicoptor rotor, a small pot-gardenia in the kitchen window, and that day's scattered clouds in a blue sky. That other day at Gordon's in Millinocket, as I remembered her standing for that moment five years earlier with the sun on her wet skin, the longing of the dream pressured up into my eyes and flushed out with a feeling of happiness. I recognized the women of the dream: they were Margherita. The slim form, the straight hair dripping at her neck, the black eyes, the same playful nature: they were the same.

I thought everything was solved. Suddenly the phone-booth no longer frightened me. I knew just how to persuade her to come up to Millinocket. I wouldn't even mention the energy. I'd just ask her to come up so we could remember the desire of that moment; I'd ask her to come up so that we could be in love again. If she got away from the jungle of West New York and lived here in the clearing like I'd been doing, if she quieted down her mind, there'd be no question but that she could remember; I was sure of it. After that water-fight of ours in her back yard, we'd started going out full speed till it was all we could do to keep her chaste; but what happened then, Margherita? Did we forget? Did we get buried by the nosey neighbors and the keeping up with the pay-ments and all the rest of the routine, or didn't we? In my mind I won my debate with her. That night I called home.

She wasn't there at first. I got her on the third or fourth try. I didn't want to upset her, so when she answered I tried to act what I thought was naturally, by saying right away: "Hey, where you been all evening? I've been trying to get you."

She didn't say anything for a minute. Then: "Joey? Joey, is that you? Are you at the bus-station? Joey?"

"I'm up in Maine, like I told you in the telegrams, didn't you get them?" She didn't answer. "Hey, didn't you get them? Where were you tonight, anyway? Is someone else there?"

"No, I was at my course, I"—

"Your course? What's this, a course on what?"

"It's a refresher, for my cosmetology license"—

She stopped talking again, so I asked her if this was for her job, or what?

"Joey, why didn't you call? Why aren't you home?" I could hear that she was crying. For some reason, I hadn't expected this; I hadn't wanted us to talk about how I had treated her very badly.

"Don't get upset, okay?" I told her. "I thought you'd be glad to hear from me."

"I am — I am."

"I had to be by myself, Margherita. I couldn't think straight when I was down there in Jersey. I had to settle some things and solve some things, and I didn't feel like I could call until things were better."

"You could have told me, though," she said. "You could at least have told me what you're doing, because it's been almost two weeks since you left and not even a phone call to tell us what you're doing."

"Okay, I know this, it's been eleven days, and I wanted to call you, believe me, I tried to, but I couldn't, Margherita."

"Just to say you were alive, though, you could have done that much, for God's sake what you put us through."

"I'm sorry, okay? I had to calm myself down, Margherita. I can do it up here. The people are quiet and real decent, and there isn't anybody to bother me. It's out in the country, with lakes and all? I got a very nice job. You'll see." I wanted to add: you'll see when you come up here and live with me. But I didn't have the courage. I was afraid it would sound too sudden. I was hoping maybe she'd hit on it herself. But instead she said: "How long till you get better, Joey?"

"I am better. Things fell into place, Margherita. I am better."

"Then can't you come home? Joey, aren't you coming home?"

"I want you to come up here first, though, just to see the place." I decided that once she was up in Millinocket, she'd be able to understand. How could I talk over the phone about the close-mouthed Yankees and the woods and the dream and being in love again? "Just to see what I've been doing, Margherita."

"Why, though? Why, if you're coming home?"

"I don't know if I'd get confused back there, that's the thing —just right away, I mean. I might need a little more time, see, but we've got to get together, because there are a whole lot of things we've got to talk about; you know that."

"I thought you were better, though? You said that, Joey? Can't you come home, then?"

"Margherita, I don't want to argue about it. I don't want to have to explain things over the phone. This is why I couldn't work myself up to call you. I just need to see you, okay?" She didn't answer for a minute, so I said, "I want us to begin, Margherita. I want us to start over again from the beginning. I know we can."

"I've got a job, too, though, Joey. I can't just take off like this, to go to some crazy place"—

"How do you know it's crazy? Just because I'm in it?"

"I didn't say that, Joey, but"—

"It isn't crazy, Margherita. I'm better, I told you. I want you to come up and see." She didn't answer again, so I pushed it: "Your boss will let you off: sure, for something like this? You can come up over Thanksgiving, and if he docks you I'll make it up to you."

"How can I get up there, though? I can't afford this."

"Sure, you just take the bus to Bangor. I'll send you the money Western Union. I get paid tomorrow, I'm sending you a hundred-twenty dollars. The pay is very good here. There isn't any problem."

She put up a bit more of a fight, but we both knew that I'd won. I practically always won our arguments.

I tried to prepare for her, though. In another widow's house I found a sunny double room looking out on the street. I bought Margherita some warm gloves and a scarf and I checked out the eating-places. I bought the Volkswagen from Gordon against my next paycheck, and I got a Maine license plate, which I thought would make me look settled. All I could think of was the memory of her standing in her soaked shirt on her father's doorstep. I stared at couples walking on the sidewalk or driving by in a car and imagined the happiness of soon being like them. In the past, I'd always considered loving my wife and child as something ordinary, something anybody should do and probably would do the same as I had, if he wasn't too hassled. But now it seemed to be something blessed; it seemed like the meaning of my life. I felt vindicated in having left West New York, since it was the coming of the energy that had opened my eyes. I spent the week of waiting in a frenzied agitation of desire.

Thanksgiving came. Margherita was already in the bus-station waiting when I got there. Right away as she stood up, I could see that she was thinner, the way she was when I first knew her. She came across to meet me: "Hey, Joey." We both felt embarrassed; we didn't know to how greet each other. She stood there holding her suitcase. I asked her: "Listen, would you take off your hat a second? I want to see how you look." She had one of those fur hats you fold down over the ears and tie by a string under the chin.

"Oh, I'm growing my hair out," she said. "I didn't even want you to notice, and here you" — She had her hair straight now and shaggy, with the ends close on the back of her neck. She looked younger. I wondered if she, too, had been trying to remember. — "What do you think of it?" she was saying. "It's got to grow out first, but it's two nine-dollar haircuts and Mr. Rosen's doing it for free, isn't that great of him?"

Rosen was her boss, the one who had thrown me out of his beauty parlor when I'd barged in there after her. "It looks real nice, Margherita." I took her suitcase. "What do you have in here, bricks?"

"Magazines. It's eleven hours up to here."

The desire that had made me sweat during the drive down to Bangor to meet her seemed to have frozen in the embarrassment and the cold night. We went to a pizza-parlor and talked a blue streak about everything we'd been doing since we'd seen each other: it was like we were old friends trying to catch up on news. We talked about Vin.

"He asks for you, Joey. He wants to know when his Daddy's coming home."

"Yeah, well we're going to fix that." I told her how my visit with Father Jeremy had been a washout. "My mind hasn't really bothered me at all, Margherita. There's nothing to make me nervous up here, except your not being here. Wait till you see the place."

"Aren't I seeing it? It looks like any other city, Joey, if you ask me, though."

"No, didn't you listen? This is Bangor. Millinocket is seventy miles north of here."

"Seventy miles? Seventy? Do we cross the border into Siberia to get to it?"

She'd already been complaining about her legs aching with the cold while we were walking to the car. I'd told her she shouldn't have worn such a short skirt, and she'd told me that she'd worn it for me and that I ought to have warned her ahead of time.

"Sure," I said, "We'll buy you some some ski-pants. You get used to it; you get to like it. It's too cold to have fights and problems. These people up here, they'd think Jersey was a nuthouse."

"There are a lot of nice people in Jersey and you know it."

"Yeah, and they all rallied around when I needed help."

We changed the subject; we didn't want to talk about any disagreement. On the way to Millinocket, she joked about whether we were going to pass any dog-teams on the highway, and did I get us a room in a motel or in an igloo? "Come on, Joey, mush! mush!" she shouted when I had to shift down on a hill. Our talk got more and more playful, and when we got to our room we got straight down to the business of marital relations, but I couldn't find the perfection and the happiness that had been in my mind before she came. It was nothing but two friends relieving each other of a burden, as a favor. The flush of being back together semed to die when it was done. We noticed that a television was very loud in the next room. I told her I'd go ask them to turn it down.

"That's all right. I could sleep with a subway next door, after that bus-ride."

"Are you glad you came up, though?"

"Well, you didn't give me any choice."

"Are you, though?"

"I don't know, Joey. We'll talk in the morning, okay?"

We didn't talk in the morning, though, since it was Friday and I had to work. We met for lunch, and in the evening we went to Gordon's for dinner. Everything was friendly. Margherita and I had always got along well on the day-to-day aspect of things. Now and then that day, I hinted at what I wanted:

"You have to admit this is a real pretty town, Margherita."

But she wouldn't give any ground. "I guess it is nice for these people, if they like being out in the sticks like this."

I'd given her some money to buy some warmer clothes, and on the next day, Saturday, I drove her to one of the lakes a few miles outside of the town. We walked through the fields toward the edge of the woods. Nine inches of new snow had fallen in the night, and as we walked, the snow began again, one of those perfectly quiet falls that you only notice when it lands there on your hand. The sky dropped a white ceiling, it seemed only a few feet above our heads, and the flakes that twisted down out of it were larger than either of us had ever seen before, half an inch across. We watched their starry shapes melt and vanish on her sleeve. "You ought to be able to keep them," she said. She lay down and patted out angel's-wings with her arms stretched out in the snow. As I watched her, the longing of desire that I had felt in the dream grew in me again. She was absorbed in her own thoughts as I watched her, and she seemed distant, someone never to be reached, as foreign as the women of the dream. As she stood up from the snow, then looked at the angel's form disappearing there under the falling snowflakes, then lay down again to pat out another pair of wings, she seemed reachable only by the power of my own longing joined by the power of hers, as if our desires were circles of force that we had to expand outward from ourselves by sheer wish, until the circles touched and overlapped. We had stepped into each other's circles almost by chance that day in her father's back yard, by lucky chance; watching her there in the snow, I was sure that we could bring our circles in touch again, if she would only stay in Millinocket and allow it to begin. I lay down beside her. The snow seemed warm; desire kept us warm. She seemed just there, just at the edge of the circle. Afterwards I thought that if we had only forgotten our bodies and made our love just then, just there, despite the wet and cold, we would have lain in our circles together. But we went back to the car, and as we drove back to town the longing drained out moment by moment till the circles dissolved, and we were just two people on a bed in a room, as it always had been.

She went down the hall to take a bath, and she spent a good while there. When she came back she turned her back to me and got into her clothes quickly. She was shivering. "I can see why you like the snow, but the cold I can't see," she said.

"Sure, but this is a widow who is chintzy with her boarders, Margherita. Most people up here keep their houses like a hothouse in winter. You dress right, that's all. I told you this."

"Okay, you told me." She came over and sat next to me on the bed with a determined look about her mouth and eyes. "Now you tell me what we're doing in this place."

"We're seeing it, Margherita. We're looking it over, since how else are we going to understand what kind of places there are besides Jersey? Like there's no reason we"—

She interrupted me: "What's wrong with Jersey?"

"That's just what I've been trying to tell you by showing you this place."

"How come you don't want to come home, Joey?" Her voice seemed very loud in the room.

"Okay, now take it easy. We're going to talk about this, so you think a minute. What do I have to go back home to, except an unemployment check and a lot of one-time friends and a bunch of nervous in-laws who worry all day about whether I'm going to cause trouble and embarrass them?"

She was already telling me: "You just watch it about my family, Joey Celebriśi, since I couldn't have made the payments this month if it wasn't for them, and I couldn't even have gone to work if Carmella hadn't watched Vin, who is your kid who you left in the lurch without any explanation and without even saying goodbye to him"—

"Okay and don't you think that bothers me?"

"Then why did you do it?"

"I had to, Margherita"—

"You didn't have to. You wanted to, for God knows what reason"—

"Will you listen to me and calm down? I want you to listen to me, Margherita. How else are we going to understand this? What I'm telling you is, if you came up here with Vin, we wouldn't have these problems. I've got good pay here and the houses are real cheap compared to Jersey, to rent or even buy. We could actually have a house, a real one-family house with a yard for Vin and for flowers like your father has. You wouldn't have to work if

86

you don't want to. There's lakes for you to swim in in summer, Margherita. And you met Gordon and Joyce; the people here just aren't nosey, and they aren't going to drive me nuts again."

She was plucking at the bedspread fitfully. "It wasn't the people who drove you nuts, and the only reason your so-called friends up here don't bother you is because they don't know you and they aren't your kind of people. If we lived up here, we wouldn't have anybody to really talk to, and we'd be climbing the walls."

"We would know people, though. We would, Margherita. We'd get to know them. You start again, that's the whole reason for this, see what I'm trying to tell you?" I was speaking quietly and stroking her shoulder, to persuade her; I was sure she'd understand if she could only see it calmly. "We can start again; I know this. That's what the whole upset back home was all for: just so we could change and bust the routine and remember and start loving each other like we were supposed to do. Do you remember that day when we had the water-fight at your father's place, when we first knew each other?" She nodded after a minute, frowning. "Well, the other day I suddenly remembered it like it had happened yesterday, like it was happening over again. I want it to be like that again now, Margherita. It can be, if we start again and just have each other."

She said bitterly in a low voice: "And what if you have trouble again, Joey. Then what happens. Then where are we."

"We'll be perfectly okay because there isn't going to be any trouble. The energy and everything else that happened was just to bust things up so we could remember and begin again; I know this. If you and Vin come up here, it's just going to be clear sailing."

She shook her head and blinked, with her hands tight in fists in her lap. "What if you get it in your head to run off again, and you leave me with Vin in this god-forsaken place, Joey? Can't you see this?"

"I could see it if there was a chance of it, but there isn't, Margherita. After all we've been through to get here? There just isn't a chance. Believe me."

She turned away from my hand. "I don't believe you."

"You've got to, though. You've got to understand."

"I don't understand. How can I know what you're going to do? I don't understand you." She got up and walked over to the dressing-table and held on to the chair with her back to me. "There's no way I can know what you'll do."

I didn't know whether I should go over to her to comfort her. I felt afraid of her. "You would know what I'd do, Margherita, if you tried to listen to what I've told you all these times, like if you ever listened about the energy and gave it a try, instead of just assuming I was going nuts, the way everybody just assumes it."

She was shaking her head. "The things you say don't make sense, Joey. They just aren't good for anything. They aren't what people have to do."

"You don't know this," I said to her, my voice rising. "You just figure you know the right way for everything, and you don't care what anybody else might want"—

"Oh, is that what you think?" she said, turning around to me very fast: "Is that the way I am, while you"—

"It is the way you are, about this"—

"And what about you? You're always trying to do for the other guy, is that it, Joey? Except who is it who left his wife and son without any warning and without any preparation? and who except all those nosey people and nervous in-laws that you can't stand — they're the ones who came around and helped me out and made the payments and cleaned the house and took care of my child, when my husband was sending these crazy telegrams from some godawful place, and I thought I would go wild with not knowing if you were safe and what was happening to me?" She was holding on to the back of the chair and leaning forward and almost hissing at me: "You say I should listen to you and understand you, but you don't even bother to ask about me, because what do you care about what's happening in my life? You don't care if I better myself or if I have a nervous breakdown and end up on the dole. I had to borrow the money for this course I'm taking, and you don't care if I pass and get my license or not. You haven't asked about it once, because you don't think about me."

"I do so. I think about you all the time."

"You think about your crazy ideas all the time, and maybe you try to work me into them, but that's not thinking about me, Joey. I want a decent life so I can be upright in front of people and have Vin grow up to be something, and I don't want him or me mixed up in your ideas, because your ideas aren't of any use. They're worth nothing."

I was stunned by this; I had no idea she had all that anger in her. She was standing over me and shaking. She said after a minute: "I'm going home and staying home whether you come home or not, and sometimes I think I wouldn't care if you just didn't come back at all."

"I'm afraid to go home, Margherita." I plucked at her skirt as she stood in front of me. I felt deadened. "I don't know if I can."

"Then stay here." She walked away and sat down at the dresser.

"If you and Vin aren't here, then I don't want to stay here either, can't you see this?"

"Then you can come home," she said in a flat voice.

"Margherita, I want you to stay here. I want you to stay here."

She sat looking at the floor and working her hands, and for a moment I thought she might agree to stay. But she shook her head and said quietly: "You come home and be my husband like before, and I'll be your wife like before. That's all I can give, Joey, even if it isn't enough for you."

I didn't know what to answer. I couldn't face carrying the logic of it any farther.

Minutes went by. After a while she asked: "Is there a movie-theater here?"

We sat through a double-feature, so that we wouldn't have to talk. Back in the room, we both lay awake for a long time.

In the morning we were carefully friendly again. We wanted to protect ourselves from any strong feeling. I didn't know what I should do about her leaving. I didn't want to think about it. We chatted our way through breakfast and the ride down to Bangor, mostly about Vin and the appealing childish things he'd said and done since I saw him last. Margherita bought her bus-ticket and we stood in line for her to get on, almost as if we didn't know what we were doing, as if we were home and I was putting her on a bus to see her aunt in Staten Island. The driver started taking people's tickets. The line moved up. She gave me a hug. "Take care, Joey."

"Maybe I can come home soon, Margherita; maybe a little longer, I can't tell."

"Sure, Joey. You see." She gave the driver her ticket.

"Tell Vin I'll see him soon," I said. "Tell him I think of him."

She got up on the first step and turned sideways to answer, and I saw her as she was on her father's back steps in the memory, and as she was in the dream. The resemblance leaped into her face and shone there. The longing of the dream burst up through me and seemed to spread out in a circle to touch her as her lips moved. The sound of another bus revving up nearby covered her words.

As she turned and stepped into the bus and moved down the aisle, it felt as if she was taking something from inside me along with her. It seemed to stretch between us, stretching thinner and thinner. I wanted to push in after her to stop her, but the entrance to the bus was jammed with people. I rushed along the side of the bus to look for her in the windows. I shouted her name. I couldn't find her. It wasn't till the driver was backing the bus out of its dock that I saw her in a window on the upper deck, talking to the person next to her, leaving the circle as soon as I'd found her there, gliding backwards out of my life.

FIVE

On the way back to Millinocket, I stopped half a dozen times and tried to work up the courage to turn around, drive south, and catch up with Margherita's bus on the highway. I'd beep my horn, and we'd shout at each other at sixty miles an hour, and she'd rush off the bus at the next station — I'd see the anger in her face, and the daydream would fall apart. All the rest of the day, the memory stabbed into my mind of her standing there shaking and telling me she was finished with me. There was no way to answer her. It was obvious that any wife would have done just what she did. I sat in my room, staring out the window at the woods till my eyes burned from not blinking. I tried to figure out how I ever could have thought she would want to move up to Millinocket and get involved in my crazy ideas. She'd always despised them, and she was right to despise them. That seemed as clear and cold to me now as the winter air. I didn't know why I had made such a ridiculous fuss about the energy in the first place, throwing up my job and my family and my home for it — just for an odd feeling which as far as I could tell nobody else had ever heard of. I didn't know what I had cared about it for; I'd never even known what it was. I'd thought it would lead me to the meaning of my life, and for that I gave up living my life. How could I be anything but crazy? How could Margherita feel anything but scorn? She seemed gigantic and terrifying to me; I wept, thinking of her.

I would gladly have changed places with anyone I passed on the street or worked with at the mill. But even if such a thing was possible, there wouldn't be anyone who would want to change places with a ridiculous case such as mine. All through the week, an agony of self-hatred tormented me, with each self-hating thought linked to the next one in a burning chain: the things I'd done to Margherita, how I'd abandoned my own kid and hurt him, how I'd bewildered my parents and made my friends laugh at me and despise me, and how they were right, I had gone nuts, I was crazy — I beat at my head to stop it from thinking these things, but how could it stop? The thoughts were true. There was nothing else for me to think of in their place. There was nowhere for me to go. The future seemed like an extension of the slope I had to climb to get to the mill, and I saw myself climbing it, carrying this worthless burden of myself, for years and more years.

At night, fits of jumpiness attacked me. I couldn't sit still or lie still for more than a few seconds. I'd get exhausted shifting and clutching myself and turning. I took the tranquilizers that the psychiatrist back home had given me, but they made it worse: my body disappeared into a stupor, and the thoughts of self-hating hurtled around in my mind like insects in a hot closed room. I took to sitting up all night and staring out the window across the dark fields to the woods, trying to hold my eyes open and to stare through the jumpiness, till at last a heavy sleep would seem to glide down off the black shapes of the ridges and over the fields, up through the window, and into my mind. Each morning when I woke up in my chair, I was still more frightened by the need to get up and to climb that slope again and to listen to the thoughts of what I'd done; and then to come back at night and face the jumpiness in my room. For half an hour at first in the mornings, then an hour, then two, then three, I'd sit there in the armchair paralyzed by my thoughts, till the pain of having to relieve myself was too great for me to sit any longer. Finally, at the end of the week, Gordon told me that if I was late punching in one more time, he would have to turn me in to management. I could see he was worried, but he didn't know how to ask me what was wrong.

The next day was Saturday, the first Saturday in December: I remember thinking that this was a new month I had to live in and try to survive. I thought how ridiculous that would sound to someone who wasn't crazy. From where I was sitting that morning, I could see the logging-trucks and hunters' pick-ups speeding towards the woods, while a couple dressed in parkas snowshoed across the fields. Their being able to work or to go out and enjoy themselves, their wanting to do things at all, just their wanting to live, were all mysteries which I must have once known the secret to, but which now I could never hope to decipher. They found the courage for living so easily, without even thinking. Their lives outside my window seemed beautiful and lost, like the life in an album of snapshots taken in someone's parents' childhood. As I thought this, the jumpiness came back, and I recognized the anxious feeling behind it: that I would never return; that I would never be able to live life again, because I had lost the desire.

Why should I live, though, if I didn't want life now? Why did I have to climb that slope, if it was too long, or have the thoughts, if they tormented me? Suddenly I wished Margherita hadn't rescued me that day in the kitchen at home, when my thoughts were scattering like crumbs, and a dark emptiness was blotting my mind out. I wished I had died; what did she mean by taking death away from me? There would have been hardly any of the disgrace, there wouldn't have been any of the fighting afterward, if she hadn't interfered. The trouble would have been over so easily. Even now, though, I could die; it could be over with. As I thought this, my jumpiness disappeared. To have died seemed as quiet and peaceful as the woods that stretched back on their dark ridges for endless miles under the sky.

Without noticing that I'd succeeded in getting myself out of my chair, without thinking what exactly I was planning or doing, I put on all my spare clothes, which bunched up on me in bulky layers so that I could hardly get my coat on over them. I told myself that I wanted to be warm when the time came. I left the key to my room on the bedtable. I drove the Volkswagen out of Millinocket and onto the main logging-road into the woods.

At first the pavement-markings and directional signs and summer house-trailers held away the presence of the trees. But after ten miles or so, the pavement narrowed onto gravel, with long fingers of ice in the ruts. Snowbanks three and four feet high closed in on either side, so the road became a trench between white walls. Pine-trees and firs and bare birches crowded down to the banks. I stopped the car and began slowly walking in among the trees. The trunks stood very close together, and the branches were all dead for twenty feet up, sticking out in sharp stumps that met and crossed like the arms of turnstiles. I couldn't take a step without my clothes becoming snagged and my face being whipped. Ahead, the trees seemed to close together in a grey-black wall. I said aloud that I was going in there, whatever the trees might want. When my voice died out, I noticed that the woods were completely still.

I knew then why the people of Millinocket huddled together in their clearing. It wasn't the cold of the woods or the snow. It was the emptiness. There was nothing there but the grey-black branches and the white snow. It could almost have been night, lit up by a very bright moon. My feet crunching and the branches cracking in my path and even my breathing sounded loud and hectic and conspicuous. Whose mind could hold itself together after an hour, two hours, after a day in this silence? Whose thoughts wouldn't scatter out and be lost among the endless trees? Sometimes a crash would come faintly from away in there, and then the stillness would flood back in again and wash over my mind like a surf. Then the surf would recede, and the hot shouting thoughts would be there again, telling me I had no right to escape, I ought to stay at my job and send money home to help Margherita and Vin, it was wrong to want to die, I was crazy, I needed help, I was crazy; but already the thoughts seemed to be spoken somewhere slightly distant, somewhere above and behind me, so that I wasn't sure whether it was me who was thinking them, or whether it was someone else talking in a memory. Only one thought seemed to be mine now: to give my life to the woods, the way I was never able to give it to Margherita until it was too late and she no longer wanted it.

Heavy clouds were moving over the trees. The air was warming, with a smell of thaw and snow. I went back to the car and drove on with the same warm feeling settling in myself, as if I was preparing for an act of love. The longing of desire struck up once again within me. I wanted to drive to the center of the woods and bury myself there and dissolve into nothing. I wanted to drive till the woods and the widening circle of my longing became one. I drove for what must have been hours, up the ridges and down again, jouncing over the icy track beside the unchanging trees. I listened less and less to the frightened thoughts, till they were nothing but blurred and scratching sounds that mixed with the rattling of the speeding car. Closer and closer the silence of the woods surrounded me, seeping first into the back seat, then next to me, then around my shoulders and head and neck, then into my emptying mind, till I could no longer tell the presence of the trees from the presence of my longing to be lost among them.

Snow began to fall. Wet large flakes clogged up the windshield. The car began to slip and whine. Above the sound of the engine, I could hear the wind rising and calling. Out of habit, I put the car in low gear and tried to keep up my speed, but soon it was obvious there would be no driving through the storm. The grey curtain of trees along the roadside slowly faded from sight, till all I could see through the windshield were white flakes driving out at me from a white cloud. It was time. I was glad. I took my foot off the accelerator and let go of the wheel. Immediately the car spun around, then floated quietly broadside into a drift.

The wind shoved at the car and howled around me, climbing and falling in a thousand voices. I thought the trees had been driven mad with longing. Other thoughts came: I should stay in the car and leave the motor running, and maybe I'd be safe, someone might be coming through with a plow — the thoughts shouted urgently across the empty spaces in my mind, and for a moment I wondered curiously who was being talked about. But I was already pushing the door of the car open against the drifts. The wind burst in howling and filled the car till I thought it would shatter outward. The next minute I couldn't remember if it was the car that might shatter, or my mind. I noticed that I was stumbling around in the road. Thick flakes whirled around in the wind so that I couldn't see farther than the length of my arm; when I shot out my arm to keep my balance, my hand disappeared into a white darkness. I wanted my hand to disappear; I didn't want to see it again. Why should I see anything but the whiteness, or hear anything but the wind? The wind and the whiteness were welcoming me. They pressed and pressed lovingly against my senses till it seemed my mind and my body were slowly parting like a fabric that had been stretched too far. Soon it would be my own voice howling; it would be my darkness. My thoughts seemed to fly out into the storm. After a little while, I noticed someone slogging around in a blizzard; I didn't know who it was. It seened to be a snapshot I was looking at. In the snapshot, someone was looking at another snapshot just like it, and in that other snapshot, a man was holding still another. As I looked, I seemed to fall down through endless shimmering photographs into a white silence.

SIX

WHEN I LOST consciousness, I fell down in a kind of shelter between the car and the snowbank: this is where two snowplow-drivers fround me. They hauled me into the cab of their truck and shoved brandy down my throat and jabbered into their radio and yelled when I started to pull my gloves off my aching hands. I didn't understand one word they said. Afterwards I realized the reason: they'd been speaking French, I had driven across the border into Quebec on the logging roads. But at the time I had no idea where I was or what was happening to me. Large patches of my body seemed to have disappeared from my feeling, and as the truck barreled through the woods, there were long silences in my mind. The drivers kept shaking me out of a daze.

Later I remember being helped into an ambulance. The sky in the window was streaked with the colors of evening. Soon up ahead, across a river, a city stood at the summit of high cliffs, with a huge old-fashioned deluxe hotel looking out from the edge. I remember I wasn't sure if I was seeing an actual place or a television advertisement, and I thought there would be girls striding across the bridge at me and swinging their hair in silence.

It was the city of Quebec. For a week I lay in a hospital, waking with a start every few hours, and looking around the room, wondering who I was. Strange things were there in my mind: shouts and monsterish faces and crowds of people in bright-colored clothes. The doctors gave me drugs against the shock, and they cleared up the frostbite on my nose and feet and cut off two dead fingers from my right hand. Then brick by brick, the house of my mind gradually rebuilt itself as I slept, till I remembered myself and everything that had happened to me a good deal more vividly than I wanted.

I had my life back and my mind, and despite what I had lost I was very grateful. I walked around that wet chill grey city, full of a childish joy at the foreign people and things I'd come alive again among — the dumpy bar-ladies and their large bright steel café-au-lait steam-machines, the red-and-white oilskin tablecloths in the cafés, the prim spiffy secretaries hurrying through the snow-flurries, the construction-workers, all small men like myself, in their blue berets. I was glad they were foreign; I felt foreign to myself. I had no idea who I was supposed to be any more. The man who had kicked away his family and who would have succeeded in killing himself if a certain blizzard had lasted longer and had kept the snowplows away longer — this man seemed to belong not just to another country, but to another lifetime. I could hardly feel him. The hurt and the longing, and the excitement of the energy, were buried in a kind of dullness. As for something new, where was a hint of it? There was just one day, and then the next and the next, each floating by in a foreign language; to survive was enough for me.

I found a job cleaning vats in a chemical factory. I dressed up in what was more or less a space-suit, climbed down into the empty vats, sprayed solvent with a hose, and scrubbed with a long steel broom. In the evenings, I sat in the café on the first floor of the hotel where I lived, and I watched the strange, jabbering, confident life flow by. It was obvious the people there all thought they knew who they were. Dumpy Madame Surtis, now, she was the lady who ran the Hotel du Clos and made café-au-lait all day with her steam-machine and served shots of brandy to her husband Jean-Hébert, the foreman at the chemical factory, when he came home after work full of racial remarks about the West Indians. That's who she was, and Jean-Hébert was who he was. Maurice the red-haired postal-clerk, who nipped in for his anisette every night at six exactly, and said "Exactement, exactement," to Jean-Hébert's complaints, he was exactly who he was. It was fixed, it was all settled. What if they were fired, widowed, crippled, deported? What if something erupted from the bottom of their minds and exploded their lives apart? Would they survive? Probably, yes; but they would be different. Then who would it be who'd survived? Who was it who lived through that blizzard and was sitting there watching them? This is what puzzled me. If I was going to begin again, I had to begin with what I was; but what was that? It was a long time since I'd thought Celebrisi was his job, his family, his hobbies, his friends, his place in his home-town, all the things Jean-Hébert and Maurice and Mme. Surtis thought they were. For me these things were long gone; but I was still here. Could I say that Celebrisi was his mind, or his thoughts and feelings, or his personality, then? It would be more comforting to say I was nothing, since my thoughts and personality and the rest of it had shifted and transformed themselves until by now I hardly recognized them. I believed that there certainly had to be something lasting to be found within myself, but as to what it was or how to find it, I had no idea.

It didn't seem to be urgent to find an answer. I was able to drift in a mild confusion. I sent part of my paycheck home every week to Margherita, and now and then there were letters back and forth from Margherita and my mother and sister. I couldn't tell them when or even if I would come home; I told them there would just have to be a wait until I could say.

The cold months passed. I learned to get along in French; the people who worked at the hotel befriended me. My mind felt slowly more secure. But the more settled I became in Quebec, the less I wanted to stay there. I couldn't see the point in building anything now; it would just be building on air. I began eyeing the Volkswagen as it rested in the parking-lot behind the hotel. One day I beat out the dents that I had made bumping into the snowbanks in the blizzard, and I tuned up the engine. I began taking drives out of the city onto the farm roads. The black loam in the bare fields was cold and rich as cake in my hands; it smelt metallic from the melting snow. In the villages, each one named for a saint and each one centered around its grey wooden church, old women dressed in black, like the Italian grandmas back home, stood in the doorways of grey wooden houses and called out to children in the street that a car was coming. In my hotel, now and then in the mornings, a sweetness in the air would slip in through my window, promising new places and new life.

Then one afternoon at the chemical factory at the beginning of April, a man in white coveralls came around from the government, tapping with his pencil on his clipboard. He got very insulted when he found out that the fellow in the space-suit down there cleaning vats was an American without the proper working-papers. Jean-Hébert was furious. He hurled down his hardhat for emphasis. Would the American do better work if he had the papers? He challenged the inspector to explain the use of an inspector's existence. The inspector wouldn't say. He tapped on his clipboard and wrote out a notification. Afterwards, Jean-Hébert offered to help me go after the papers, but I was glad the government had forced the issue. It was time to move on. I wanted to go south towards the spring.

But not south towards Jersey. I wanted to know something, at least find something out, before I thought about going home. I drove southwest along the St. Lawrence River, through Montreal, then into Ontario, then back across the border into Michigan, onto the American plains.

The flatness of the plains amazed me; it was the landscape inside myself. The black plowed furrows shot out across the fields to the horizon without a single hill to break their aim, not a rise even, nothing in the way, so that when I stopped the car on a back road and stood up on the roof, I stood in the center of a vast circle, as bare as my own life. In a minute a pick-up truck jumped up from behind the horizon and zipped along a dirt road, spitting mud behind. I watched it cross the circle and drop off the edge again. As clouds moved, sunlight revealed tiny upright slivers of a new crop that covered the field in front of me with a green down. I stood on the roof and day-dreamed about travelling all spring, about looking for myself, about criss-crossing the bare plains that hinted at growth — Indiana, Illinois, Iowa, Minnesota, Kansas, North Dakota — the names resounded like promises in my mind.

I knew it wasn't possible. I would have to stop and find another job. I hadn't kept much money from what I'd earned in Quebec, and also the Volkswagen needed some welding work and a couple of new parts in the engine. The next night, on the Indiana Turnpike not far from Chicago, the car suddenly lost power. The fuel-pump had given out even sooner than I'd expected. I parked on the shoulder, and the car rocked with the wind of the trucks roaring by. I looked out over the flats between the turnpike and Lake Michigan, where shapes of immense factories stood darker than the night against the sky. Plumes of bright orange flame flew up from them. The idea of another marginal job in a place like them made me feel pretty weary. A state cop swerved up and told me I had to get my car towed. I didn't have much money left after that.

At the state employment office, they told me they had nothing for me in the steel mills — the fiery places I had seen beside Lake Michigan. But they said there was always some turnover at the packing-house in East Chicago. I didn't even ask what the packing-house packed. I figured I'd be lucky if I kept off the dole. The East Chicago city bus wound through neighborhoods of two-story red-brick houses. Then it dropped me at the gates of a black fortress of smokestacks and piled-up cookers and block-long sheds with sooted-over high windows. A blackened sign rose from the highest roof among the smoke. I could just make out the brand-name of the breakfast-sausage that Margherita would sometimes buy for Sunday mornings. What they packed was meat; it was a gigantic slaughterhouse.

"Where were you last week if you wanted production mechanic?" asked the steely-haired woman in personnel. "You can sit on the line," she said, "or you can leave your name."

"Anything you might have, Ma'am."

She looked wearily at my application-form. "I have a place in Building Five." She put me on the assembly-line to pick pituitary glands out of hogs' heads for the minimum wage.

It was actually a disassembly line. There were forty or fifty of us, women mostly, sitting on high steel stools around a bench that ran around the four black walls of a huge high-ceilinged room. Slow three-bladed fans drooped down from above, and iron walk-ways scattered this way and that over our heads. Various super-visors and occasional troops of visitors led by a little man in a white coat tramped over us on the walkways.

A conveyor-belt was sunk into the bench in front of us. In rode the pigs' heads, looking waxy and solemn. Each person was assigned a certain bit of anatomy to rip out of each head as it passed by. The backs of the heads were gone when they got to me. Using a long pair of curved scissors with a blunt guard, I had to nudge aside the brains and snip-snip, pluck out the pituitary, a bright pink pea. Five peas a minute, that's three hundred an hour, twenty-four hundred in an eight-hour day till I ached with the burning stink of the place and my head was a blur. Who could look around in his mind after a day such as this? I rented a room in the red-brick neighborhoods, in the basement of a family's house — I hardly even noticed their names at the time — and I leased a television and flopped down in front of the comedy-shows every night in a drugged daze. The job even ruined my habitual hamburger dinner. The animal juice bubbling around my teeth made me retch, and I had to switch to pizza and peanut-butter sandwiches.

I told myself I'd quit this lousy business as soon as I'd built up some cash and fixed my car. But long before I was near that point, I got used to the slaughterhouse. The stench of it no longer bothered me, and the pituitary-snipping became so much of a routine that I'd get completely lost in my thoughts and forget where I was for ten or fifteen minutes at a stretch. The I'd suddenly notice myself there, snipping away like an automatic machine. It was obvious that this was how the steady workers stood the job. They just naturally shut off their minds. Since they were hired to be machines, they lived up to the idea. At 8:00 a.m. they came in as people, and inside of ten minutes they were transformed into rows of automated arms with tools sprouted out, jerking down at the pigs' heads in a perfect rhythm, while their unnecessary minds wandered off into noplace.

My hands in their routine fascinated me. Down, shove brains, snip pea, up, plunk in pail — down again, shove, snip, up again, plunk: my hands moved themselves without my telling them, as if they weren't my own. As I concentrated on them, the energy began buzzing silently in my shoulders and under my scalp. It took me by surprise: I hadn't felt it for months, not since Thanksgiving-time, in Millinocket. I had long since come to think of it as part of a phase that was past. Yet here it was, seeming no different now in the slaughterhouse than before in North Hudson Park and in the snow, radiating from my skin and making me feel warm and light. I felt wary of it, and I told myself to ignore it, since it had been extremely adept at getting me into trouble. But at the same time I opened myself to it with a feeling of welcome. I continued to concentrate on my hands, and the burning grew on my skin, then died out, then returned. It turned on and off all that

104

afternoon. I left work feeling invigorated and relaxed. The television shows seemed stupid. I went upstairs from the basement and for the first time struck up a friendly conversation with the couple whose house it was.

I took the return of the energy as proof that my mind had begun to repair itself. I was getting well; maybe I could begin again. Of course for all I knew, the energy was getting ready to turn my life inside out again. But I decided to let it happen. I had hardly anything to lose this time, except the energy itself.

It was as before. As I concentrated on my hands over the next few days, the energy would gather slowly upwards through my body, flowing up my spine and across my shoulders, then up through my neck to push hard from underneath against my scalp, at the same spot a couple of inches in diameter, just behind the center of the top of my head. The flowing energy seemed to want to push open some barrier there and to escape upwards into the air. But not to escape from me: instead I felt it wanted to escape with me; it wanted to carry my thinking mind with it, away from my physical brain. It seemed possible. Why couldn't it transport the location of my thoughts, since it was already transporting my power of senstion? As the energy rose up through my body, I could no longer feel my legs, then no longer my stomach nor my chest nor my arms; they were lost below my shoulders in a burning glow. All my sensation was crammed into my head and neck. I thought I must have pulled up all the energy that normally lived down lower in my body, where it was used for normal feeling.

It was all extremely intriguing to me. I only began to worry that my hands would make a mistake as they worked. The real danger was that my mind would run off with its thoughts about the energy and forget to pay attention to what I was doing. Soon enough, the sad-eyed lady who sat next to me was nudging me with her elbow and talking to me; but for several moments I found that I couldn't grasp hold of my attention and move it to listen to her words. Her face was puzzled and concerned. She was pointing to my hands. The blood on them was thicker than usual. Suddenly the thought spoke in my mind: She's probably telling me I've cut myself. Immediately I felt the energy bolt back down from my head into my body. The second finger on my left hand suddenly ached and stung. The sad-eyed woman had already called the supervisor. He was behind me, saying: "You'd better get to the nurse with that. Over in Administration, you know where?"

He took my seat. As I walked out of the building into the courtyard, wrapping my finger in my handkerchief and squeezing it against the pain, the thought occurred to me: Why should I bother to feel this? I wasn't feeling it before, was I? I stopped walking and concentrated my stare on the smoke floating up from a nearby stack. The energy began flowing again, and I found that by willing at it, I could pull it up faster from my body than before. The pain in my hand was lost again in the glow. The space of my mind filled more and more tightly with the energy till I thought the barrier at the top of my head would have to give way to the pressure. Suddenly I felt that my body was lower down from my mind than before. Without my noticing it happen, the energy had expanded around the top and the sides of my head. The pressure was gone. I could feel the energy burning there in a sort of round shape, but elongated and a bit pointed at the top, with vague borders all around. It seemed to be flowing quietly outward, as if with rays of an invisible light. The point of my consciousness had moved upward within it, to just an inch or so above my head. My thoughts rattled on, noticing this, noticing that, but everything else was still. As I crossed the courtyard, I couldn't feel my feet on the cobblestones. My body seemed to weigh nothing at all. I thought I could have walked for days.

After that day, I kept the energy in its ordinary place in my body, for safety's sake, as long as I sat on the line at the packing-house. But in the evenings and on my days off, I was jealous even of the time it took to eat; I wanted nothing else but my experiments with the energy, as I called them to myself. On the wall of my basement room, there was an out-of-date calendar with a photograph of a lake in Minnesota. I took it down and stared at it for concentration. If I concentrated hard enough, I would forget about eating or drinking or any other business of my body, because I couldn't feel my body. I was free of it while the concentration lasted. It was the same with anger and feelings of sexual desire and the attacks of longing for home: I could escape them, too, for a while. The stronger the feeling, physical or emotional, the more stubborn the concentration I needed to pull the energy out of the feeling; that was all. I decided that it was the energy that gave the feelings their power. The feelings were the electromagnetic systems of my human machine, and like any other electrical system, you could pull the plug on them. You sapped them of their power by concentrating on something else. When the energy was no longer circuited through them — this is how I explained it to myself — my energy automatically flowed up into its natural place around my head, where it seemed to be at rest.

The experiments elated me. The idea that I could control my feelings gave me hope that I could avoid any new disasters like the one in Millinocket. But this progress revealed a new barrier, a disturbance in my concentration that I'd never taken account of before: my thoughts. Trains of them would ride across the field of my mind and take my attention off with them. When a series of thoughts had exhausted itself, I would suddenly realize that my concentration was lost. The energy would be dispersed. I would have to begin over agin.

I started listening to these thoughts of mine: I realized that I had never stopped to listen to them before. It was embarrassing to notice how trivial they were. But when they came riding along, something forced me to take my energy and board them and hold on with both hands for dear life. It was infuriating. I wanted to drag the energy out of them, I wanted to order them down from my mind, the way I'd done with the feelings in my body. But they belonged to a different kind of system than the feelings, and I couldn't figure out how to disengage myself. It seemed inconceivable, after all, to be separate from my own thoughts: who was it who would be separate? I realized it was the same problem I had run across in Quebec, just put in new terms: I didn't know where among all these electromagnetic systems of thoughts and feelings was myself.

Whatever I was, I was obviously becoming more and more of a somewhat peculiar character. The possibility of my ever going home was every day becoming slimmer than a communion wafer. But I told myself it was all right; it was all right. Let me be the person who didn't know what he was. At least I had the energy. I would work on getting free of all my systems and on becoming light and still. Back home they'd thought this was all crazy, but I was beginning to think what actually had driven me crazy was not the energy at all, but the newness of it and the confusion and the ripping away of my old life. But if working on the energy was crazy, let it be. It did nothing but make me more at ease and more peaceful, and as far as I could tell more sane.

The more peculiar I allowed myself to be, if that was what it was, the odder other people looked to me. They were all of them ordered around by their feeling-systems; they hated their systems and they believed in them. They were led around like bulls by the nose, and most of the time they took it without a murmur. This made me feel superior as I thought about it, but it also made me angry that people just like myself should be pushed around like this. I considered the family who lived upstairs from me to be a particularly pitiful example. By then I'd become pretty friendly with them: Birlak, their name was, Ned and June. He had thick black eyebrows and black hair that stood up straight like a bristle-brush; his job was to push a pencil in the purchasing department at one of the steel mills. His wife June worked the cash-register in a shoe-emporium in a shopping-center. She had a very round blond face and was one of those women who are always looking around vaguely because they're too vain to wear their glasses. Ned and June had a thirteen-year-old son named Lonny, dark like his father and tall for his age, already taller than his parents. I never found out why there were no other children.

Lonny paid for being an only child. His mother was possessed by the nightmare of losing him to pneumonia or the traffic on 141st Street or the tough boys in the ninth grade. She was always fussing and hovering and fluttering over him and adjusting his clothes and warning and reminding and telling him. He thanked her by making the kind of sharp sarcastic remarks that kids his age are sometimes very adept at. Ned, the father, didn't take sides in this. All he wanted was for them both to be quiet. He'd pace up and down the house getting blacker and blacker under his black eyebrows till I thought he would blow up the house with the force of his frustration. June knew she was infuriating her son and her husband, but she couldn't stop; the fussing-system had taken her power away from her. I'd watch the pressure-head of fussing-steam burst out of her even as she tried to hold it in. I believe that she had once fussed over her husband, but that it had somehow transferred itself to the boy; and now she was too afraid of her husband to transfer it back again. I think he wanted it back, too, but he was too confused and too proud to ask.

Ned and June still shared one thing in harmony: plants; flowers. The house was thick with green leaves, hanging from the ceiling, on windows, on shelves; and the frontyard, backyard, sideyards were a crowded garden of flowerbeds and shrubs and ornamental trees. June took me around for the grand tour. I remember her pointing to some green blades that were fattening at the top with unborn blooms. "Iris," June said. "Now these will be the yellow-and-white. Ned,"she yelled, "What are the yellow-and-whites? By the water-meter? I'm showing Joey?"

"*Ad astra;* yellow hafts and standards, white falls and beards," came his voice from behind the house, where he was building a greenhouse off the family-room.

"He knows all the names," she told me. "He's always wanted to own a nursery. I just wish he'd do it."

It was the beginning of May. I helped Ned pour concrete and lay the steam-pipes for the greenhouse. As we worked, he poured out complaints about his year-in-and-year-out pencil-pushing at the steel mill. He said he couldn't afford the pay-cut of just working for a nursery, and he couldn't take the risk of borrowing on his life-insurance to go into business for himself. "There's all this," he said, nodding towards the house, and meaning his nervous wife and his smart-aleck kid and the mortgage and the payments on the car and the clothes-dryer or whatever. It was plain to see that his wife would have moved into a four-room apartment and gone to the laundromat without a complaint, just to have him come home content at night. But he couldn't see it. His anger had closed his eyes.

I felt sorry for them. It wasn't like my own marriage, since these people didn't have any basic disagreement about things. They were just caught in some bad systems. This made it even more pitiful. I was very tempted to try and persuade them to take up concentrating every night for half an hour on a Christmas-cactus or something, so they could calm down and build up some energy and look at themselves for once. I thought if they could get out of their fussing and anger systems for just once, even for a minute, they might be so amazed at the feeling of freedom that they'd resolve to try to get out completely, over the long run. But I knew that if I spoke about it, they'd just think I was crazy.

They almost never went out together in the evening. June wouldn't leave Lonny home by himself, and he made a terrible fuss if they tried to slap a sitter on him. He never went out with friends — I don't think he had any — he kept to himself, like a lot of kids his age. The three of them spent every evening in that house, saturating the air with negative force. Lonny had a passion for fighter-bomber airplanes. He had models of them stacked on

110

clear plastic shelves all around his room, as thick as his mother's house-plants in the living room. He had books on the subject, full of photographs and diagrams, and he knew all the names, specifications, speeds, maneuverabilities, heroic pilots, and the famous bombing-runs of history, complete with casualty-counts and degrees of destruction in terms of dollars. He'd re-enact them in his room at night. I could hear him above me there, imitating dogfights and explosions. He'd lecture me on it, with his dark eyebrows frowning to make sure I didn't interrupt or doubt anything he said. A certain amount of the statistics I believe he made up. I liked him. He was a nut on his subject, as I was on mine.

I wanted to try to rearrange the energy in that house without letting on that I was doing it. I hit upon a plot. In a hobby-shop in the Near North Side of Chicago, I bought the components of an electric motor, and I told Lonny I'd show him how to assemble them. He fell for it. The very next night we had the components laid out on the floor of my room in the basement. When it was assembled, we hooked it to a grindstone to sharpen his father's garden-tools. Naturally, the motor made a trip to Lonny's eighth-grade science-class, and he came back with a note full of praise from the teacher. Before long he had out a fat book on electromagnetism from the high-school library and was lecturing me on the various principles.

"That's real fine, Lonny," I told him, "but you have to understand it in your hands, too. Your father knows all the gardening rules, now, but he'd be nothing without the instinct."

"I have the instinct," Lonny said. "I have lots of instinct."

"Sure, I think maybe you do. If we took the motor apart, for example, do you think you could reassemble it?"

"Sure I could. That's easy." he said.

It wasn't easy, especially since he didn't enjoy getting advice, and after the third evening of failure at it, he spent a couple of hours in his room doing bombing-runs. But he was as basically stubborn as his teacher, and on the fourth try he put the motor together. "We're doing a short-wave radio next," he said.

"Okay, but first we fix this old hot-plate I picked up, so I can cook without bothering your mother."

"Yeah, my mother," he said, with poison in his voice. "Let me see this hot-plate." He looked it over. "This is nothing."

His parents hardly saw him now. Lonny and I even ate dinner in the basement among the wires and components and tubes. One night Ned took his wife to the movies. Then it was the flower-show on Sunday, then the greenhouses at the University of Chicago. Some of the tension that went out the door with them didn't return. I was pleased with myself. I called it my Birlak-stunt, and I wished that I'd had the sense to do stunts like this one when I'd been home.

Eventually I couldn't resist trying out a few of my ideas on Lonny. I thought that since he was young, his mind wouldn't be set against something that might sound unusual. I warned myself: here you are listening to your wanting-to-explain-it system again, and it's always gotten you nothing but trouble. But the desire to pass on what I thought I knew was too strong.

"People operate according to electromagnetic principles of their own, did you ever think of that?" I asked Lonny one evening.

"Sure I did. What do you mean?"

"I mean people work by means of systems, and they power the systems with their own personal energy."

"Oh, yeah. This thing isn't working, Joey." He was trying to tune our short-wave radio.

"For example, like your mother," I said. "You get mad at her for fussing at you, am I right?"

"Naw, I'm not mad at her."

"Well, I'd say you sometimes get mad at her, but here's why you don't have to: this fussing-habit of hers is just a system she's got herself caught in. It isn't actually her, see, any more than the tuning-dial is the whole radio. If the tuning is busted, what do you do? blame the whole radio?"

"It isn't the dial. We need an antenna."

"I told you we need an antenna. You're smart, Lonny; you already know the principle. You mother fusses because her fussing-system isn't tuned right: it goes on too often. You ought to get angry at it, not at her, because she isn't the same as it."

"Yeah, she makes me sick."

"The reason you get sick is your own anger-system, which is tuned to go on every time she fusses at you. Every time it goes on, it makes you uncomfortable. You ought to do some work on it. Adjust the tuning a bit. I'll show you how, one of these days."

He was studying the radio intently. "You're screwy in the head, you know that?"

"Oh yeah?" I didn't like hearing that.

"Mm-hm, my father told me. He says that's why you don't have any family or friends or anything." Lonny gave me a satisfied look. "Think he'll buy us an antenna?"

"What's this 'buy'? We can make one."

It annoyed me to find out that the Birlaks had already decided I wasn't normal, when I hadn't even mentioned my ideas to them. Obviously they'd been speculating about me during all those weeks when I'd sat alone in my room after work. I was sorry I'd even hinted to Lonny about the energy. I hoped he would forget about it. Instead he adapted it to his uses immediately. The next day after work, there were heavy feet on the stairs as I sat there staring at my picture of the lake and trying to clear the pig-stench from my head. In his short-sleeved white shirt, Ned stood leaning forward in the stairwell, frowning at me.

"Would you mind telling me what you're teaching my kid?" he said.

"We're still on the short-wave radio. We're going to put up an antenna, if that's okay."

"Would you like to know what he said to his mother this morning?"

"Sure, what was it?"

"He said he didn't have to listen to her, because Joey said she was just an electromagnetic system."

"That isn't what I told him, Ned."

"Oh? Just what did you tell him, if you don't mind?"

"I tried to explain to him that June couldn't help fussing over him sometimes, so there was no reason for him to get mad at her." Ned was glaring at me. I went on: "I said habits get ahold of people, almost like they're electrical systems working inside, and there's no point in getting mad at an electrical system. Sort of along those lines."

Ned studied me for a while. "Well would you mind sticking to motors and radios and keep out of my family affairs?"

"Yeah, sure, Ned, no offense, hey."

I expected some sharp parting remark, but instead he waited around for a bit, looking at his feet. "Listen," he said, "We've been planning to go up to the lakeshore over Memorial Day. A place up in Michigan. June and I. Would you look after Lonny while we're up there?"

"Sure, be glad to."

He nodded. "I appreciate this. You can forget the rent for a couple of weeks." He waited a moment, then turned around to climb the stairs, shaking his head. "She said Lonny told her she needed to be sent back to the factory for repairs."

I hadn't heard the last of it. A few days later, Lonny came downstairs and said: "Listen, hey Joey? When you take apart the hogs at the packing-house, are there wires inside them? transformers, stuff like that?"

"Am I supposed to laugh?" I asked him.

"Not actual wires, stupid, I mean"—

I interrupted him: "Don't call people 'stupid'."

"All right, I mean is a hog a kind of machine, though?"

"It's got systems. But it's alive, you have to remember that."

"So what difference does that make?" Lonny said.

"It makes a difference. Which isn't what you told your mother the other day, I hear."

"My mother. Being alive doesn't make any difference."

"Yes, it does."

"What's this big difference, then?" he said.

"I'm not actually sure. Living things power their own systems, for example, and machines don't."

"I already thought of that," Lonny said scornfully.

"So good for you." I picked up my lake-picture. I didn't want to bother with him.

"The hogs have to be born to get charged," he said. "They have a battery-cell. When it runs down, they're dead. It's just a difference in how they're manufactured, that's all."

"You know what you've told me? You've told me that you aren't able to say what the difference is yet."

"You don't know," he challenged me.

"I'd like to know, Lonny, and if one of us finds out, we should tell the other person right away."

"I want to see the packing-house."

"You asked that when I first came here, and you know what your father said."

"So what, I'm older now, and I have a good reason."

"You mean besides enjoying all the blood?" I said. "One big bombing-run?"

He refused to be nettled. "It's a scientific reason. To see."

"The blood's all you'll see. You think your father has a lousy job? Besides, you can't answer questions like this just by seeing things, Lonny. You have to look at yourself."

I figured I'd had the last word with that, but he ignored it. Young or old, the last thing people want to look at is themselves. "I want to take the guided tour through the packing-house," he said.

"You ask your father." The truth is I didn't want to take the tour myself; I didn't want to know what I was involved in by

115

working there, any more than I had to know. "Your father's the boss around here," I said.

"Yeah, all right."

"And this time don't put words in my mouth."

"Yeah, all right."

He didn't mention it again for a couple of weeks, and I made the mistake of forgetting about it. Ned and June were busy instructing me about the details of the house and the routine of plant-watering so that nothing would die or collapse during their few days on Lake Michigan. They were in a nervous fever. June told me that it would be their first weekend alone together since Lonny was a year old. Watching them load the car, I suddenly felt sorry for myself. But I consoled myself: Look, you're watching the culmination of the Birlak-stunt. You're doing better.

Once June had finished with her last minute instructions and her make-sure this and her make-sure that and her hugging Lonny till he squirmed, and once Ned got her out the door and into the car and they drove off, Lonny remarked mildly, "The tour's at ten o'clock, Joey."

"What tour?"

"Through the packing-house. Tomorrow. It's your day off, isn't it?"

"Did you ask your father?"

"Mm-hm, yes I did."

"And what did he say?"

"He said okay if we went together."

Lonny was looking at me with a very innocent expression, and so I didn't actually believe him. But it was too late to check on him, unless I called up his parents at their motel that night, and I didn't want to humiliate the boy. Besides, I thought a good sight of gore might shock him a little, and that idea pleased me.

The tour began in a bright clean room lined with dioramas setting forth the anatomy of the hog and the history of meat-packing in America. There was a grocery-corner with the products of the place and a display of pharmaceuticals that use animal derivatives. The display was pill-bottles pouring out from a red plastic pig's mouth. A small man with a high voice and a sharp face, dressed in a white medical coat, came in and lectured us: 'The Hog: Beneficial to Man'. His name was Crosby. I'd seen him from my seat on the job, leading tourists across the iron walkways overhead. There were about a dozen of us on the tour that day: three or four older couples on cross-country trips, and a pair of bearded college kids from Fort Wayne, who said they were in the neighborhood visiting their grandmother. "Any questions?" said Crosby. "Follow me, then. Please keep to the marked walkways. Do not run."

We tramped on the walkways from huge black room to huge black room, each given over to dismantling another part of the hog. There were quartering rooms and tanning rooms and lard-boiling rooms and gut-drying rooms. Lonny pretended to be taking it all in with cool interest, but I could see that his stomach was turning just a bit, along with the rest of them. Crosby kept soothing us by pointing out how clean and efficient the place was. "You know what those long white strips on the stretcher down there are, my young friend?" the tour guide said to Lonny: "Intestines. Guts. Miles of them. That's what makes the jacket on your breakfast-sausage. Didn't know that, did you? I thought you didn't." This went on for close to an hour. "They say we use everything but the squeal. If you could think of a way we could use that, you could patent it and be a rich man," Crosby said. "Any ideas, anyone? How about it, my boy?" I have to admit I was just a bit pleased to see Lonny without an answer for once. He was looking rather pale.

Suddenly there was the faint sound of squealing, and Crosby herded us into a waiting room full of green furniture and photographs of waterfalls. He gave a little speech about how the last part of the tour was a little strong for some people, and anyone who wanted to sit it out right here, please feel free to do so; the

117

room was fully air-conditioned. The old ladies and the college kids decided they'd all had enough touring for the day. The old guys were ready, though. "As for you, my friend," Crosby said to Lonny, "young people have to be fifteen years of age to see the slaughtering-room, so I guess that means a parting of the ways. We have *Field and Stream* and *Popular Science*, on the table there."

"Oh, no, thanks," Lonny told him. "I'm fifteen years old and three days. This is part of my birthday."

He must have planned it in advance. It was possible; he looked old for his thirteen and a half. The tour-guide looked at me. I was feeling queasy, and I didn't want to fight over it. I also didn't want to admit to Lonny that I'd just as soon sit out the slaughtering-room myself. I told myself: Fine, I hope it really upsets the kid. I said to Crosby, "It's like Lonny says."

The squealing of the hogs sounded half-way between the screaming of horses and the screaming of women. It blasted at us when Crosby opened the door to the slaughtering-room. We had to cover our ears against the noise. It was another black room, slightly smaller than the others. We filed along a walkway twenty feet above the floor. Through a tall gate at the far end of the room, the fat brown hogs were being prodded into a chute one by one from the stockyards outside. The hogs flailed in a panic to climb the sides of the chute, but they couldn't get a grip with their hooves. As each one blundered out from the near end of the chute, two men, one on each side, reached down, wrestled with the hog a bit, then snapped a clamp on each of its hind heels, and the clamp swung the hog suddenly upwards to a moving chain eight feet above the floor. Hanging upside-down by its hind feet from the chain, the hog rode across the room, jerking and squirming till it seemed it would break its back. Its open screaming mouth flashed at us. Two shirtless brawny men stood just below us, with long knives in their hands. As each bawling hog drew near, one of the two men snatched it by an ear, swung up his knife, and sliced the hog's throat half through. Blood jumped out in a wide rope and splattered over the slaughterers. Then twitching and spurting, with its head flinging half off its moorings, the hog rode off through a door on its way to the dinner-plate.

It made me feel sick to think that I had been taking a hand in this murdering. I wanted to get out of that packing-house and never see the sight of it again, and never see the sight of meat again. I completely forgot about keeping an eye on Lonny. Suddenly there was a commotion on the walkway. The tour-guide pushed past me and let out a yell. Lonny was running back towards the door that we'd come in. One of the old men was stumbling on ahead of him, retching his guts out. Before Crosby could catch up to them, Lonny slipped in the old man's vomit, pitched forward under the railing of the walkway, and fell twenty feet down to the floor below, just behind the nearest slaughterer, in a wash of blood. The boy's face turned up to us, twisted in fear and pain, with his mouth wide open; we couldn't hear his yell over the hogs' screams. Crosby hurried down a ladder with me after him, and he shut off the power to the chain. When we reached Lonny, the slaughterer had already cut the boy's right trouser-leg with his machete and was ripping it up to the crotch. The leg was bent in the middle of the thigh. But the skin wasn't broken. Lonny was sobbing with fright. The last hog twitched just above us on the halted chain, flinging blood on us. It was hanging stock still and staring by the time the ambulance-drivers came in with the stretcher. Then at the hospital, the doctors kept Lonny waiting in the emergency room for three hours before they got around to him.

While we waited, I told Lonny about the hilo-race and my own accident, so as to get his mind off the slaughtering-room and to show him that his broken leg luckily wasn't very serious by comparison. He didn't want to hear about it. He didn't want to talk to me. He lay there chattering. I had to go down to the nursing-station and yell, in order to get a blanket for him. I cursed myself for agreeing to take him to the packing-house and especially into that last room. I'd wanted to get back at him: it was shameful. A kid that touchy, at that upsetting age; and I had to take advantage of him. I told myself he'd probably go back to his bombing-runs with a vengeance now. I sat there watching Lonny and waiting for the surgeon, alternately badgering the nurses about the delay and cursing myself for still being a complete incompetent with people and always ending up by wrecking things and hurting people, despite all the progress I thought I'd made.

I'd left word by telephone at Ned and June's motel on Lake Michigan, and soon enough towards evening, after the doctors had straightened Lonny's leg out and put it in a cast, there was June half-running down the aisle of the hospital-ward, with Ned charging in behind her. June was weeping and scared out of her wits. She ran up to the boy in the midst of telling him it was all Mommy's fault and she'd never leave her little Lonny ever again. I believe I felt worse about hearing that than about any of the rest of it. Ned was pacing up and down the aisle and yelling at me: "Well what happened? They wouldn't tell me what happened."

I told him what had happened. "It was a clean fracture, Ned. He's going to be okay."

That set June to weeping again, which exasperated her husband. He cursed me, his face pale under his shadow of beard. "What did you take him to that place for?" he said. "Didn't I tell you to stay home and work on that radio?"

"The kid said you gave him permission, Ned. I should have called up and checked with you. It was a mistake."

Ned turned on Lonny. "You hear what Joey says? You're going to get it, mister, believe me, before this is over."

"Stop it, Ned, stop it," June was saying.

Lonny turned his head away from her and said quietly: "I didn't want to go to the packing-house. He made me. He wanted to show me the hogs are different from machines, and they aren't. They're the same."

June yelled at me, "How can you talk to a child about these

120

things?"

"Take it easy, June," Ned said. "This is a hospital."

"The kid's upset," I told her. "He doesn't know what he's saying."

She went on in a quiet voice: "You came into our house, and we didn't care about where you'd been or what kind of trouble you'd been in, because we believe people should have as many chances as they deserve, but when you start talking about all your disturbed ideas to my child"—

"All right, June, all right," Ned said.

She shouted at him: "You're the one who said there was something wrong with him, and you let my baby get mixed up with him"—

A nurse and three orderlies were pouring down the aisle at us. "It's all right," Ned told them. "We're taking care of this. Joey, will you —?" He nodded towards the door, and the two of us walked out the ward while June called after us: "You just get him out of my house, Ned Birlak."

In the hallway we stood against the wall, out of the way of traffic. "Listen, Joey"— he looked at the floor. "Whatever she said, will you forget about it? because I think you've been good for Lonny, you've been real good for him"— his voice trailed off; he was shaking his head and sweating.

"Look, I don't want to cause any more trouble," I said. "I feel terrible about this. As soon as my next paycheck comes in, which will be Tuesday, I'll clear out, okay? and she won't have to bother with me."

He had already interrupted me and was saying furiously: "Don't you listen to what she says"— He cursed her.

I tried to calm him down a bit by saying, "She was right, though, Ned. If I hadn't been happy to see the kid get disgusted, I wouldn't have let him into the place, probably."

"It's not your fault, Joey, and I'm not going to let her pin it on you." He went on after a moment more quietly: "Something had to happen. If it wasn't this, it would have been something else. She'd have found something. She'd have spoiled it somehow."

"She's going to slow down, one of these days, Ned. The kid's going to grow up. She's going to let him go."

I'd touched the raw spot. He was shaking his head again and weeping. We didn't talk any more.

SEVEN

I STAYED another two weeks at the Birlaks' house. June spent most of her time with Lonny at the hospital, and so I hardly saw the boy at all, since I didn't want to get in her way there. Ned came downstairs several times to talk to me. What had happened seemed finally to have let him admit to himself that something had to be done about the problems in his life. I tried to find the right words to encourage him to look at himself.

"The woman needs help," he said one night. He had come home late from work, and we were eating together in the basement. June was still at the hospital with Lonny.

"How are you going to tell her that?" I asked him.

"I don't know. She won't listen to hardly anything I say to her right now."

"If a person doesn't believe he needs help," I said, "Then he won't accept any. I know this from my own experience, see."

Ned gave me a sharp look, as if it had suddenly occurred to him that I might have a past he could compare with his own.

"You could suggest that you both go for help," I said. "As a married couple."

"Yeah, I don't know, though." He was frowning.

"You'd have to admit that you also need help, the same as her."

He didn't answer this, and I didn't know if he'd accepted what I'd said. But later he told me he'd discussed things with June, and she'd agreed they could use someone to talk to. They were going to set up an appointment with a counselor in the county health department. I never found out if they went, or if it began to help them. Once Lonny came home from the hospital and June was home in the evenings, I could see I'd be likely to turn into an obstacle for them, since she saw me as being on Ned's side. It was time for me to go.

I was glad. I'd had more than enough of the slaughterhouse. But besides that, alongside the hope that I felt for the Birlaks, a new hope had begun for myself. After all the damage I had done at home, I had now actually succeeded in helping somebody a little bit, while keeping myself out of trouble. Though for a lot of people this would have been something very ordinary, for me it was a passage over the boundary from negative to positive; it was a kind of graduation. I'd passed because of the energy; there was no doubt of it. The concentration exercises had taught me how to keep calm in the face of upset and emotion and to understand the confusion when the Birlaks were too confused to help themselves. The only mistake I did make was to let Lonny see the slaughtering, and I'd made it because for that one day my anger had got the best of me.

I wanted to be alone again. I wanted to work all day every day on concentrating my mind and on building up the energy until nothing would be able to push me off course, until I could control my feelings and thoughts as completely as I could control my own hands. Maybe this was an odd goal, but it felt right to me. It elated me. It was my finest stunt and my work.

Soon before I left East Chicago, Margherita wrote to say that she was selling our house and she had moved up to Fairview in Bergen County into an apartment with a divorced woman she had met in cosmetology school. "I can't afford the payments, Joey," she wrote, "and I guess I don't believe you're ever coming back now. I have to make my own life." This shook me, but I got back into my hopeful mood after a day or so. I signed the house-papers and sent them back.

"I don't know what the energy is," I said in the letter I wrote to her, "and I don't know why it had to come and change my life and your life and Vin's. I just know that it turned my eyes around 180 degrees so that I began to see what's inside of me. This is what I'm living for now, to keep looking and looking into my own mind. Don't ask me when the looking will be over, because I don't know if it will ever be over, or if there is any one end for me to get to. It's not like looking for a ring that's missing in the upholstery. It's looking for my real self, and the truth about my life. This is what anyone is really after, and I'm not different from you, basically. It's just that you look for yourself in the family and the neighborhood life, and I had to leave, so that I could learn how to look inside myself.

"Maybe you still think this sounds crazy — I guess you probably do, but I know now that it's the opposite of crazy. Concentrating your mind and working up the energy, which is what I do, makes a person feel very solid, very pulled together, because your different feelings and thoughts are brought together into one piece, like iron filings onto a magnet. You feel that you are just exactly right here. But when you go crazy, it's the opposite. You don't know where you've gone, because your pieces are busted apart and scattered all over the room. You can't get your thoughts and feelings together at all. I know this from the time I lost my head in the kitchen at home, and I had a worse time in Maine after you left. What I think now is that the craziness came from my being pulled and torn apart when I had to chose between you and the things that were happening inside of me. This shouldn't have had to happen. I could have stayed with you and Vin if there only had been someone to explain to us what was happening to me. It's wrong that people don't know about these things. It's wrong that you all had to think I was crazy and that this did help drive me crazy for a while. The energy is a good force which can help people. I know this now. What I don't know is how I can show it to you, but I'm going to keep on trying to find out, so that someday I will have something to give back for all the trouble I've made for you and Vin."

I left the Birlaks and drove for two days west, across Illinois, across Iowa, into the Dakotas. The cold brown plains that had seemed clear and empty to me in the spring were now warm with crops, gold with wheat and green with the unripe corn. The cornstalks waved their tassels like cheerleaders in the wind. Where was I driving to, through all this gaiety? It suddenly occurred to me that I didn't know; I hadn't even thought about it. I let the car drift to a stop by the side of the highway. Why drive anywhere, why drive at all, since it was my mind that I had to travel in? Besides, I thought, the longer I drive the Volkswagen, the sooner my cash is going to run out, and I'll be forced to find another job and pour my thoughts outside of myself onto routine things.

I drove into the college town of Mitchell, in southeast South Dakota, and put two want-ads in the school paper, one to sell my car, and one to buy a used sleeping bag and backpack and the rest of the gear which the young travellers who I'd picked up as hitchhikers always carried. I sent half of what I made on the car to Margherita, with a note that there'd be nothing more from me for a while.

Selling the car, the last important object that I owned, seemed like the final act of leaving my own class of people, and it frightened me for a while, even though I'd never gotten along with my own class of people. With my thumb out and a sleeping-bag riding on my shoulders, I kept having thoughts about what Margherita would think or what my father would think if they

126

saw me on the road like this, looking like a hippie. Finally I gave into my feelings and ordered a U.S. Marines' style haircut in a barbershop in a town which consisted of fourteen weatherbeaten buildings dozing by the railroad tracks. In the midst of the haircut, I burst out laughing at myself, startling the old barber so much that he gave me a nasty nick in the ear.

It was the middle of June; the winter wheat was ripe in the fields. I hitchhiked north on the gravel roads, following the harvest, sometimes riding with a farmer on his way into town in his air-conditioned Pontiac or Buick, sometimes walking all day with the high wheat on either side of me, till it seemed the road was a dusty ship-channel marking an old course through a golden sea. I stood up on the roof of an abandoned car and watched the wheat flow everywhere over the flat lands, with nothing to break the surface but a line of hedge that rose here and there like a green shoal. A combine-reaper was harvesting at the edge of the round horizon. I could just see the glint of the afternoon sun on the window of the cab. The little smoke of its diesel stack puffed like a freighter's stack against the sky.

I walked in among the wheat. The ripe heads scratched my hands. Then the wind rose, and I watched it sweep across the surface of the wheat, bending down the top-heavy stalks as it came, making a deep golden trough of a wave that sped across the fields. The hiss of it whispered around me. Then the wind divided into criss-cross gusts, and the single wave broke up into hundreds that scattered and collided as if in consternation. The heads of grain knocked against each other with a clacking sound. But nothing was lost; nothing had changed. The wind died, the sun sank; the wheat stood in its place and was still. As I watched, I knew it was this that I wanted for myself. I wanted to accept the thoughts, the feelings, the other people, the winds of life, but at the same time not be uprooted from myself: to be awake, but be still; like the wheat, to give, but not to move.

In North Dakota, just above the South Dakota line, after I'd been walking and hitchhiking for about two weeks, one of those square grey International Harvester vans stopped for me in the morning. A little stocky man sat propped up on straw cushions behind the wheel. "Morning" was all he said as I got in. His looks immediately intrigued me: he obviously wasn't a farmer. He wasn't wearing a hat, and he had a square head too large for his body, with short stiff black hair shooting this way and that in spite of the hair-oil that shone from it. The hair-oil touched the air of the van with a greasy sweetness. The little man could have been fifty or seventy; wrinkles were gathered on the pale skin by his eyes and below his ears, but his hands were clear. He had soft and rather fat fingers with clean neat nails, which made me wonder what he was doing in the country, especially in that cheap green suit a bit too small and in that pleated white shirt and a string-tie, too, with a turquoise clasp in the shape of the double letters: 'TT'. I looked in the back of the van. It was piled to the roof with flat grey boxes. This was the answer. "Are you a salesman around here?" I said. "That is, if you don't mind my asking?"

"Certainly not, young feller, certainly not." He reached back and tossed a grey box onto my lap without taking his eyes off the road or his foot off the accelerator. Folded up in the box was a pile of pinkish hosiery. "Ladies' things," he said, "toiletries, bath soap, hair oil, cosmetics, and eau de cologne." He leaned over to me confidentially. "Specialty playing cards. Picture magazines. George Terry's the name."

"Joey Celebrisi."

"What's that now?"

"Celebrisi. You can call me Joey."

"I might at that."

"You travel, is that it, Mr. Terry?"

"Indeed I do, my friend. In the summer. Eastern Dakotas, western Minnesota, eastern Manitoba. I travel the farms."

He had a high, sharp voice that filled the van with much more resonance than you'd expect from a man his size; and he rolled off his lists of places and goods with the drama and satisfaction of a caller in a bingo-game. I wanted to hear more. To keep the conversation going, I explained that I was seeing a bit of the country after quitting a job in a packing-house.

"Never went into those places," Mr. Terry said. "Smelt them."

I advised him against paying a visit. "If you went into one like the one where I worked, you'd have to give up eating meat to save your stomach."

"Would I, now? Is that a fact." And he began a series of little whines on in-taken breath, with his square chest bouncing up to his chin at each whine. I realized he was laughing.

"Don't laugh," I told him, laughing myself at his laughter, and I described the hog-slaughtering process. I said the only decent alternative was cheese-and-tomato sandwiches and peanut-butter — pizza if you could get it. "Otherwise you're eating dead bodies all the time. You're eating the casualties in a war."

I was feeling pretty fanatical on the subject by then, and since he didn't answer me right away, I was afraid I might have offended him. I was about to apologize when he said, more or less to himself: "Yes sir, that's real original. Real original." He shot me a sharp sideways look. "What'd you say your name was?"

For half an hour he sat there without speaking or moving, but smiling a small private smile, and now and then darting sideways glances at me, like people will do when they're perfecting a joke they've just invented. I had the feeling that I shouldn't interrupt him. He barrelled along the gravel roads at close to sixty, and a hurricane of dust blew up behind us, with stones clacking and ringing on the chassis underneath. I watched the shadow of the car sail beside us along the golden fields. I half-forgot that Mr. Terry was there. Suddenly he cracked out with his sharp voice: "My brother Tom, now. You never knew him. Well"—

"No sir, I didn't."

He let the disturbance of my interruption settle, and then he said: "Tom was like a father to me, as I was the child of my parents' old age — may God rest the lot of them." He rattled over a cattle-grate and passed a farmer's Buick. "Now, Tom was a vegetarian."

"Oh yeah, he was?"

"Indeed he was," Mr. Terry said.

"Well, of course, I'm not actually what you'd call a formal kind of vegetarian, I'm just not eating meat ever again if I can help it, but that's very interesting about your brother." Mr. Terry didn't answer, so I added: "So how did he get started on this, do you know?"

"I'm fixing to tell you about it, young man. That is, if you want to hear the story."

"Sure; I'd be interested."

He waited a second. "Now maybe you didn't know, if you haven't heard about Tom Terry before, but all his life, until the time I'm telling you of, Tom was famous all across the Dakotas for his rabbit stew. Even his missus stood aside when Tom took it in his head to cook up a mess of rabbit, and *her* rabbit stew won the bake-off at the state fair two years running, even though the rules confined the entries to fruit pies."— Mr. Terry interrupted himself. "This doesn't offend you, now."

"Oh, no. Go on, no problem," I said.

"But Tom's stew, my young friend; *Tom's* stew; well, I never had a taste of it; he stopped making it before my time. I do know that on the day Tom broke his shotgun over his knee and said he'd killed his last rabbit, there was an insurrection in the valley of the Cannonball which might have gotten dangerous if Tom hadn't cooked up a new stew good and fast out of turnip and greens. They had to admit that the new stew was better. As for the recipes, he never let on about either one. All he'd say was, 'Eat up before the juice dries and the fork sticks to your plate.' You never could get anything out of Tom, except when he was pleased to tell you."

Mr. Terry didn't stop to explain why he was telling me this story about his brother, or how I was supposed to take it. He sat behind the wheel, still as a stone except to dart a sideways look once or twice to see if I was listening. His high clear voice filled the van.

"Now when Tom was still a fancier of rabbit, he'd just pull on his wading boots and step across his fields to the banks of the Cannonball River, lined with thickets of cottonwood trees. He'd barge into the current and wade upstream, hollering, splashing, yowling, bellowing, generally raising a vituperous racket, and singing bits of hymns at the top of his voice — he had a fairly large voice for his size of man. I'm not going to tell you of the time he challenged a Montana grizzly to a roaring contest and deafened the poor beast. He was so sorry afterwards that he took the bear to the ear-doctor in Minneapolis. But that isn't part of this story. — As you'd expect, the rabbits who were busy nibbling the seed-pods at the tops of the cottonwood trees along the river-bank — the rabbits being particularly fond of the topmost seed-pods, which have the softest cotton in them — this diet being the reason why rabbits have such particularly soft fur, even now, though they gave up their tree-living, cottonwood-pod-munching ways long ago — as you'd expect, when these cotton-picking rabbits heard Tom Terry's racket come hollering and splashing and yowling and roaring and vituperating up the river, they never failed to stop munching and to push aside the silver cottonwood leaves, each with his right hind foot, and they'd take a look below. You know how extraordinarily curious their nature naturally is; at least, it was. What did they see but a thirtyish, fortyish, fiftyish feller in dark blue coveralls with a red woollen shirt on and a yellow straw hat; he had a big drooping moustache the color of his hat and little sharp eyes the color of his coveralls, and blam-blam-blam-blam-blam! inside of five seconds he had five brace of rabbit plummeting through the air on the way to his rabbit-pouch.

He was a wizard with a shotgun, Tom was. His mother told me once that the day he was two years old, he shot out the candles on his birthday-cake with the corks of two vinegar bottles, at a distance of fifty yards. She may have been exaggerating; I couldn't say."

Would I ever know enough to talk about the energy in the completely confident way this salesman was telling his tall tale, or whatever it was? He'd just launched into it breezily without any ceremony or any assurances from me. He didn't care what this hitchhiker with a backpack and a U.S. Marines' style haircut thought of him. He'd stopped looking over to see if I was listening; he was listening to himself. He went on:

"Well, a dry year came to the valley of the Cannonball. The stunted wheat rattled in the fields. Tom Terry found himself hollering his way up the Cannonball River two and three times a week to fill the bellies of his family. You'll understand me when I tell you that the rabbit got steadily scarcer as a consequence, and every day old Tom had to wade farther up the river to fill his pouch. One dry afternoon, far up the river, he took a turn into a bend that he didn't recognize. He told me afterward he could have sworn the river ran straight all down that country. But there was the river curving, in the shelter of a tall grove of ancient cottonwood trees. Their silver-leafed branches reached across and met far above the shaded water. As Tom was drawing breath to begin his hollering, he distinctly heard someone calling out his name behind him.

" 'Mr. Terry?'

"Tom looked around; he couldn't see anyone.

" 'Hallo, Mr. Terry?'

"There it was again, coming from somewhere above him: the high voice of a girl or a young boy.

" 'Speaking,' boomed Tom, and he scanned the trees for the source of it. After a minute, he noticed a shaking and a rustling high up in a particularly tall and stately cottonwood which stood at the apex of the riverbend. Hopping down among the silver leaves from thick limb to thick limb was a large jet-black rabbit, with particular white hieroglyphical markings on his cheeks and his brow.

" 'That Mr. Terry there?' came the high, rather squeaky voice again. It was the rabbit's voice; there was no disputing it. The sound came from where the rabbit moved, and his mouth formed the words. The rabbit hopped to the ground and walked up the bank toward Tom, using just his two long black hind feet, kicking one foot up in front of the other. 'Mr. Tom Terry?' said the jet-black rabbit.

" 'Himself,' said Tom, from the middle of the river, with the current rushing by him. He was too dumbfounded to say more.

"The rabbit kick-walked up the bank till he was opposite to Tom, turned sideways to show the white markings around his right eye, and said in his high, rather squeaky voice: 'Fire away, sir'."

The storyteller's chest jerked up to his chin in little whines of delight. "It's not that Tom had a slow mind, now," he continued. "I wouldn't want you to think that was why he stood there speechless, his arms hanging slack at his sides and his shotgun-butt trailing in the water. It was just that he wasn't used to seeing jet-black rabbits with particular white hieroglyphical markings on their faces, or any other color of rabbit for that matter, except a brown sort of grey, or maybe a grey sort of brown, and he wasn't used to seeing rabbits hop down to the ground and kick-walk up the riverbank, and he wasn't much used to hearing them talk English, either, especially dictionary English. In fact he'd never seen or heard tell of any one of these things. But Tom wasn't the kind of man to show his consternation for long, if he could help it; it didn't sit right with his principles. Mrs. Tom used to say that when the tornado of '33 snatched up their house and set it down politely on the top of the Grant County courthouse, then snatched the house up again and set it down home where it belonged, except slightly skewed around, Tom didn't even bother to get up from his dinner to look out at the sights flying by below. His knee trembled a bit on the way down, according to Mrs. Tom. But Tom denied it. 'I always did want the kitchen facing the barn, so I could hear the cows better while I was eating,' was all he'd say about it.

"The rabbit stood patiently on the riverbank, without the faintest touch of trembling about its black nose. 'Well, Mr. Rabbit, sir,' old Tom said at last, pulling himself together and bowing politely — he told me afterwards that this was how he guessed a man ought to talk to a talking rabbit. 'My mother used to say, my boy: "Tom, if you don't know who he is, then he's your better",' is how he explained it. — 'Well sir, Mr. Rabbit,' said Tom then, 'If you'll excuse me, I don't believe I can shoot you. Not like this, in cold blood; it ain't right.'

" 'I beg your pardon,' said the rabbit rather sharply. 'Is that how your mother taught you to insult strangers? I believe my blood is as warm as any other rabbit you've shot down recently. I'll thank you to aim, sir.' The rabbit turned his profile again.

" 'No offense meant, Mr. Rabbit,' Tom said, stowing his gun under his arm. 'But I'm not going to do it. A man has his principles.' Compared to Tom when he had his mind made up, his plow-mules were fickle.

" 'Indeed,' said the rabbit, in a very polite, interested sort of way. 'Just what are these principles, Mr. Terry? if there's no offense in asking?'

"Tom wasn't a talking man, and he was getting a little impatient. 'You don't shoot game that can't defend itself, if you've got any self-respect, Mr. Rabbit,' he said severely, thinking maybe the rabbit should have known this without being told.

" 'I believe I'm beginning to understand now; this is extremely educational,' the rabbit said. 'If I don't try to defend myself, then you can't shoot me; but if I try to hide or run away because I don't want to die, then you can shoot me. — Do I have it right?'

"I told you Tom had a stubborn mind; but I also said he didn't have a slow one. 'Don't you go and try running off,' he told the rabbit, 'with the idea it would get me to shoot you, because it won't do you any good.' And he hurled his shotgun onto the riverbank opposite and crossed his arms on his chest.

" 'On the farm, now,' the rabbit said, seeming not to notice, and with an air of someone trying to get a thing clear in his mind, 'before you slaughter a calf, say, do you require it to run around the pen a time or two, perhaps? or maybe butt you a little first — not in a way that might hurt either of you, of course?'

" 'Mr. Rabbit, I'm not a man for words,' said Tom, with the air of someone who'd had enough of a thing. 'I just know my ground when I see it. We'll have turnip.'

" 'In that case,' the jet-black rabbit said, 'I'll take my leave. I wouldn't want to be the one to jeopardize Tom Terry's reputation for keeping his word.' The rabbit turned around, kick-walked his way back along the bank to the tall and ancient cottonwood tree at the apex of the riverbend, hopped onto a low limb, hopped onto a higher limb, and was gone among the shimmer of silver leaves.

"Tom walked home that day without knowing he was doing it. 'The cool air under those trees put me into a kind of sleep,' he told me afterwards. It wasn't until he got home, and Mrs. Tom asked him why he was out in the garden digging turnips when it was time to cook up some rabbit, that he suddenly remembered what had happened. He told Mrs. Tom about it, and she asked him if he wasn't feeling well. She might have persuaded him he'd dreamed it all, too, if he hadn't noticed the next morning that the butt of his shotgun was warped. You remember I told you that he let it trail in the river when the jet-black rabbit first dumbfounded him by talking to him. 'I had to go back and find him,' Tom explained to me afterwards. 'Here I'd been wondering all my life why rabbits live in trees, and when I had a chance to find out, I forgot to ask. Besides, you never could tell: maybe the rabbit knew what the cows talk about in the barn at night. I was always wondering about that one, too.'

"So Tom trudged up the river again. But the bend with the grove of tall ancient cottonwood trees wasn't there to be found. Tom walked miles beyond where he thought the bend had been, and miles back again, but the river ran straight all down that country. He looked up and down the valley of the Cannonball for three days. At every particularly tall or stately cottonwood, he stopped and called up the trunk: 'Mr. Rabbit, sir! If you're there, I would be mightily pleased for some polite and peaceable conversation!' Or he'd say: 'Mr. Rabbit, sir! I've been thinking over what you said! I don't have my shotgun with me, just take a look!' He'd hold up his hands to show they were empty. But no squeaky voice came in answer.

"From those three days Tom came back home a sore-throated and a weary-legged and a changed man. He never shot a living thing afterwards; he wouldn't have a gun in the house. 'I can't know who I might shoot,' he told his missus. 'It might be him.' At night you could sometimes hear Tom out in the barn, chatting with the cats and swapping stories with the cows. If you laughed about it, he tended to get testy. 'They'd talk to you, too, if they thought you'd listen,' he'd say. Nobody missed his rabbit stew. The fame of his savory turnip-and-greens stew spread far into Montana and east across the Minnesota line. Mrs. Tom said it was the dill she'd spied him sneaking in from the garden. But he wouldn't admit to it. 'I save on buckshot,' was all he'd say, 'and I never felt better in my life'."

The salesman stopped speaking. I wanted more, and I waited for him to go on; but he was silent. Finally I asked him, "So did your brother ever find the rabbit again?"

"Hm?" He hadn't heard me.

"That isn't all there is to the story, is it?"

George Terry seemed to remember himself. "That's all for the moment, young feller. But you say there's more to it, do you?"

"Well, I don't know, you're the one who's telling it. I certainly never heard it before."

This set him to laughing again. But he didn't answer me. He seemed lost in his thoughts.

To get him to talk again, I asked him if there were many people who travelled the farms as salesman the way he did.

"Oh, there's still a few; up and down, over the line into Canada, I'd say quite a few. Not too many know the tales, though; not too many." His look turned inward; then he nodded firmly. "Now in my grandfather's time, before the radio came, and even in my father's time: I can tell you it was different then. All the best travellers brought the tales along with their wares. Some of them didn't even condescend to sell goods; no sir, they lived on their art. My uncle James Terry, now: he used to ride the Great Northern. I rode with him sometimes, back in the thirties. He'd work the winters as a stevedore on the St. Louis docks, and in June he'd quit and head for the farms. Paul Bunyan, Pecos Bill, Febold Feboldson, the saga of Brigham Young, all the tall tales of the plains: he knew them all. He'd strut up and down before the fire, or in the hay-barn if there was a crowd, and he'd play every part, switching from one to the other quicker than the eye. People would pay, then. They won't now. Although I doubt you'll be asked to pay for your dinner tonight, if you're still riding with me."

I asked him if his uncle had told the Tom Terry stories. "I guess there are more than one?"

"There are sixty-one, not counting the Osagoosa stories. You'd have to say there are sixty-two now. As for my uncle James reciting Tom Terry, he couldn't. Tom's my own invention."

"No kidding? You don't get them from books?"

He beamed with pleasure at this. "No, I only tell my own. My grandfather Norton, who taught me how to tell the tales, now he could recite hundreds of them, *and* he did his own. Sioux stories, most of them. He had enormous red side-whiskers. I told my first

Tom story to him, when I was twelve." Mr. Terry was silent for a while, chewing his lip. "It's rare as hen's teeth these days," he said. "There's a fellow out of Cutbank, Montana: he's got his own set of stories about the copper mines. He's getting old now. He pumps gas for his pay."

I said after a minute: "How do people take to the idea of a talking rabbit that lives in a tree and such things nowadays, though? If you don't mind my asking?"

He turned round to me for the first time: he had a wide clear face and grey eyes. "Why, I don't know, my friend. You're the first man to hear this one. You heard it being invented, didn't you know that? And how do you take to the idea of a talking rabbit that lives in a tree?"

"Well, sure, I guess" — I didn't know what to say.

He turned back to the road again, laughing his intaken laugh with delight. "Yes sir, you've inspired a new chapter of Tom: new and clean. I thought it would all be old ones this summer. It makes a man feel young."

We had been driving for nearly an hour without stopping at a farm; but suddenly Mr. Terry said: "Reach behind you, if you'll be so kind" — he flipped open a spiral notebook on the seat — "and fetch me one of those grey boxes of hose, with the number '5' on the label and a number '3' box also, and a box with the yellow label, number '4', and a box with the brown label, number '14'."

I rummaged among his boxes as he slowed the van and turned down a long driveway. The wheat raced past close by the fenders. Ahead, a square white house with a nearly flat red roof stood sheltered by a grove of slender trees. The van rattled across a creek on a wooden bridge; then the trees were overhead. A wind was hissing through their pale green leaves. Like shoals of darting fish, the leaves flashed their undersides of pale silver.

"Are those cottonwoods?" I asked Mr. Terry.

He looked. "That they are."

"What about your brother, then? Didn't he find the rabbit?"

"Hold your horses, young man. The lady's at the door." He dismounted from his van, carrying his boxes under his arm. He called out: "Morning, Mrs. Anderson."

A wide woman with curlers under her scarf stood in the shadow of the doorway. "Well, Mr. Terry, now I know it's summer. I've been looking out for you; yes I have."

"And how's the master? And Betty Lou?"

We spent the rest of the morning and all the afternoon barrelling up driveways ten, twenty, twenty-five miles apart, to square white houses with red roofs that stood in the shelter of cottonwood trees, and he toted his boxes up the front steps to the women of the farms. They all knew him; he knew them all and the names of their husbands, their children, their parents, their grandchildren. They invited him in for coffee and cake, which he refused by reason of his waistline, and then they gossiped on the doorstep. "Young Fred Pearson, down by Orrin," he'd say, "has signed up for another hitch."

"Has he now."

"I heard it from his mother just this morning."

"Well, I bet she's proud."

Whoever in southeastern North Dakota was married, hired, in hock, in the clear, trying a new crop, or gone to Minneapolis or Omaha, Mr. Terry picked it up like a dustmop and shook it out at the next stop, without missing so much as a name. At just the right moment in the ritual, there'd be a small pause and a motion of his arms, and the boxes would be open one by one. He knew what they always bought, and he had something new to tempt them with. He entered each sale in his spiral notebook afterward.

"Mr. Terry," I told him, "You aren't just a travelling salesman, you're a travelling social page."

He thought a minute. "I am, at that." He leaned over to me confidentially and advised me: "Don't tell Sears."

Between stops, he invented more of the story of the rabbit. He said that so many people came to hear of this man Tom Terry who talked to animals instead of eating them — like the journalist who came up on the train from St. Louis to ask impertinent questions, and the fancy lawyers for a meatpacking house in Kansas City who went to federal court to stop Tom from cooking his turnip-and-greens stew — that Tom bolted himself up in the cowbarn, saying he'd talked to his last human being. He stayed in the cowbarn for two weeks; for three weeks; the harvest was coming; he wouldn't budge. Mrs. Tom finally had to call in Osagoosa, the Sioux medicine man, who coaxed Tom out by an ingenious trick; it had something to do with making Tom believe that the cowbarn had moved, as I remember. Osagoosa was the hero of Mr. Terry's second set of stories, and for my benefit there were side-references to numerous marvels. Afterwards there was a monumental week-long battle between Tom and his wife's cousin Febold, who was tired of turnip and wanted rabbit again. At the height of the battle, the jet-black rabbit returned and politely asked Febold to shoot him. I don't remember exactly how it ended, except that the rabbit won everybody over by discussing recipes. He had an especially terrific parsnip-and-carrot soup. Then he disappeared again. Mr. Terry went over the whole story two or three times. He said he wanted to get it straight and smooth in his mind. Although it changed with the retellings, to my ears it ran smooth as water each time he spoke it, perfected immediately by the practice of fifty years.

All the warm afternoon, I listened in the van and then waited in the front yards of the farms, swinging back and forth in the old tires that hung by ropes from tree-limbs, or feeding bits of bread to white ducks bustling around the duck-ponds, or picking around the grandfather tractors that were rusting out their old age behind machinery-sheds. I dreamed through the heat in Tom Terry's world. I wanted to forget, for a while, my own confused real world, and Mr. Terry had the power to replace it with his own. Of course, soon enough I came back to myself; but what about him?

To him, I thought, his imaginary brother must be more alive than anyone else he knew: he had lived with Tom Terry not for an afternoon, like I had, but for a lifetime. Ordinary real life was a distraction to him; it was a detail. He bought and sold lingerie, but he invented a world, and his best delight was to give it away, with no conditions attached to the giving, with no questions asked. He was just exactly himself; then who could rattle him by not accepting his gift? By ridiculing his tales, who could diminish him? He was free, and his kind of freedom was what I wanted for myself.

Still, I started getting nervous for him when he told me he would launch his new story that evening before an audience of local people. He invited me along. — "That is, if you don't mind hearing about Tom again."

"No, sir, I'd be interested."

"There'll be refinements, my friend; there'll be refinements."

Near dinnertime, he turned off the highway and drove down a mile of dirt road to a town of maybe thirty white houses. Over them, like a stern old aunt who'd been too tall to get married, a grey wooden grain-elevator stood fifteen stories high, with a small replica of itself perched like a hat on its peaked roof, to house the pulley machinery. There was a wooden Lutheran church in the town and a gas station with the kind of pump you wind up by hand to return the dial to zero. A single paved street ran beside the tracks, and facing the tracks and the grain-elevator there stood a line of half a dozen wooden commercial buildings, each with a peaked roof hidden by a rectangular false front. The largest was a hotel called 'The Colorado Inn.' Seeing it, I remembered the farm women asking Mr. Terry where he'd be staying that night; he had given them this name. We went across the lobby and through swinging slatted doors to the restaurant and bar, to be seated in the center of the room by the very large proprietor himself, who served us our dinner free. As night fell outside, the room began to fill with farmers and their wives, dressed for an evening out, in string ties, collared sport-shirts, jeans, clean boots;

in print blouses, pastel slacks, and open-toed shoes. Some came over and greeted the storyteller, always as "Mr. Terry." They ordered dinner or coffee or whiskey. The proprietor brought in more chairs. Then the room was quiet, and Mr. Terry told them the story of the talking rabbit who offered up his life to teach a man not to kill.

I watched them listen. They listened the way I had listened, to forget themselves. Soon enough they stopped shifting in their seats, crossing their legs, ordering drinks, smoking cigarettes. His high clear voice held them. It became the only sound in the room. They listened not as if the tale was a children's story, but as if it was true, and as if its truth was more vital to hear than the truth about ordinary things. The golden valley he held in his mind was a valley in their own history. He invited them there, and in their minds they went. They forgot the work their minds ordinarily did; they forgot their bodies. When he had finished and they felt the absence of his voice, then their minds snapped home like an elastic band that had been stretched and released, and for a moment it hurt. I could see it in their faces. They looked up: they remembered they were sitting in the restaurant in the Colorado Inn.

But where had they been when Mr. Terry's voice held them? If I'd asked them the next day, they'd naturally have said that they'd been sitting right there in the Colorado Inn. They'd have said Tom Terry's farm in the valley of the Cannonball was only something in the mind, and where the mind goes, what the mind sees, these things are not real. Where the body is, they'd have said, what the eyes see: only that is real. But for three quarters of an hour, they hadn't believed it. For that time they knew what I had guessed from the energy, but what I hadn't quite believed myself until I saw it that night in the listening farmers: that the mind can leave the systems of the body; that it can be free in its own places; and that its places are real and have no limits, except what are set by the mind itself.

142

I went outside. Standing by the railroad-tracks, I looked up past the silhouette of the grain-elevator to the brilliant stars. Thick as lands, they filled the dark ocean of the warm night. I remembered from grammar-school another children's story, about a Greek soldier who was sentenced by the gods to wander for eternity among the stars. I thought of him up there, rowing, maybe, across the black straits between those two bright star-islands, or resting at a harbor in that constellation, crossing that diamond continent, then setting out again across that long sea, his sail bellied by the winds of space. There, was that his beacon? Who knew what distances there were in the night? Who could tell what distances there were in the mind, what continents in it and constellations, what sun might rise and flood it with light? I thought to that wanderer: if we travel together, brother, who will be the first to reach his destination, you the ends of space, or I the bottom of my mind?

EIGHT

T EN DAYS LATER, near the town of Casper in eastern Wyoming, I caught a ride with a Basque sheepherder. Soon after we drove off, his brand-new pickup-truck caught fire in the engine. I helped him put the fire out, and after a trip to town, I rewired the shorted circuit for him. He was a little leather-faced old fellow who thought the whole procedure was very satisfying. The truck belonged to the ranch where he worked, and the breakdown meant an afternoon off for him. As we worked, I asked him about his life. In answer, he drove me up forty miles of dirt road, across the high plains. The light tan land was empty but for small scattered mounds of tough grass and dark bushes and sudden high pastel cliffs, alternately pink, yellow-brown, and blue, in ragged stripes. Sheep grazed in dry canyons, where water from the spring snow-melt survived in brown pools in the gravel creekbeds. The sheepherder said the ranch covered seventy-three thousand acres; the owners were a group of doctors in San Francisco.

The road ended in a wide canyon. The ranch-buildings were strewn out among trees beside a live stream. It was July now; the sheep-shearing was well over. The old sheepherder told me that they usually hired someone afterward to check through the machinery, but no one had been hired yet. He took me into a small air-conditioned office to see the manager. Behind the desk, a fellow about my age leaned back in his chair, touching at a twirled waxed moustache which made him look like an educated wild boar. A diploma from a business school in Seattle hung behind him on the panelled wall. He peppered me with brisk questions and hired me for three weeks.

Sheep-ranching is work for loners. The ranch was a company of silences. No one took an interest in anyone else's peculiarities. When I asked the cook to make extra bread for me and no meat, all she said was: "Extra bread, no meat." People who like rules and family life kept away from those empty lands. Outside the canyon where the ranch headquarters lay — outside on the high plains, among the dry bushes and sudden winds and dust, the tumbleweed bowled like thoughts down a vast stillness. Above the monotonous land, it was the sky that changed. The social doings that ordinary people are always watchful of were replaced for the sheepherders by the sky's doings: piled thunderheads, mysterious lightning, roofs of ribbed clouds, infinite stars. They called it the weather, but they were afraid of it and half-worshipped it.

One of the sheepherders' amusements was to make suggestive remarks to the cook — Karen, her name was — a solemn person in her middle twenties. She had a long horsey face, with a long downward nose and a long upper lip that seemed to come to a point at the middle, all emphasized by long straight brown hair. She never gave the sheepherders an inch, not a millimeter,which was why they enjoyed making their remarks so much. I worked mostly around the ranch buildings, where the machinery was, so I often ran into her. Several times I noticed her behind the kitchen, sitting bolt upright with her legs tightly folded up and her eyes closed while she muttered to herself. It intrigued me; I had never seen anybody sit that way before. What was she muttering? Finally I went into the kitchen while she was cooking and asked her about it.

"It's something I'd rather not discuss," she said, not turning to me.

"So just tell me a little about it. Are you praying?" This had just occurred to me.

"Praying? No."

"I'm interested in these things," I told her. "I wouldn't discuss it with the sheepherders."

But she wouldn't be coaxed. I didn't intend to drop it, though, and the next day, when I spotted Karen at it again, I just sat down near her and tried to fold up my legs the way she had hers. Her feet were pulled up on top of her crossed legs, left foot on right thigh and right foot on left thigh. It was clearly impossible. With one foot on top, not two, my hip immediately shouted at me, and my knee sprang up in the air. She sat there ignoring me while I struggled with it. A trace of annoyance was touching at her closed eyes: she was obviously trying to concentrate on whatever she was muttering to herself, despite the noise I was making, and probably despite the pain her legs must be giving her. I remembered the fat little lady who forgot her arthritis while she knelt and recited Hail Mary's in the chapel at Father Jeremy's monastery. But Karen here had said she wasn't praying. For lack of anything else, I sat there reciting the Hail Mary. It seemed that when I sat bolt upright with a straight spine, the energy rose up faster through my body than usual.

A few minutes later Karen was looking at me and frowning. "What are you reciting?" she said.

"The Hail Mary. It's all I know."

Sun was in her eyes; she shaded them with her hand. "Why do you want to think about Mary? Do you like her especially?"

She was goading me just a bit. I told her I didn't want to have any thoughts while I was concentrating, but that it wasn't that

146

easy. "Usually I try to concentrate on a photograph I have of a lake."

"I've never heard of anybody doing that," she said.

"I just hit on it. I don't know if it's right."

"You ought to use a word."

"What word is this?" I asked her.

"It doesn't matter what word." She unfolded her legs a little gingerly. "Just so long as you don't know what it means."

"Just so long as I *don't* know what it means?"

"Mm-hm, just a sound. So you can flow with it, that's all." She stood up. "I have to cook."

I didn't know what she meant by "flowing with it," but I didn't want to risk annoying her by pressing questions on her too quickly. I had no idea how much she might know. But it was clear right away that she knew something I didn't. As soon as I tried concentrating on the sound "ah" as I spoke it in my mind, I could tell that concentrating by listening was easier. When I'd tried to concentrate by staring, my eyes got tired physically, and what I looked at would often lead my mind to distracting thoughts. A pure sound leads back only to itself. I had been trying to concentrate on the photograph for spells of fifteen minutes; with the sound, I found I could go for half an hour, although I couldn't sit bolt upright, even with just one leg folded, for more than a couple of minutes at first. During the next few days, the longer I pushed myself to try to listen to the sound in my mind, the more peaceful and awake I felt afterwards. I tried different syllables; some seemed to be easier to hear than others, and to open my mind to the energy more quickly. Reciting a single sound seemed to quiet the ordinary thoughts that always tramped across my concentration; the sound seemed to soothe them. When I recited it and then stopped, a silence without thought would last a long moment, then another, then another, and with each moment the energy burned harder and its stillness spread wider in my mind. I began to think I'd been wrong to assume that my concentration was developing the stillness: instead it seemed the stillness must have always been there in my mind. Thoughts and emotions and the business of life had been hiding the stillness from me. As I recited the sound, the stillness would wash like calm water into the narrow harbor between one sound and the next, and for a moment between the headlands I could glimpse the sea. It spread out across the distances of my mind. Perhaps it spread beyond my mind; perhaps I was the one who created the horizons. But I couldn't look far. I had to recite the sound again quickly, even though it divided me from the very stillness that it brought close, because if I stopped reciting, the ordinary thoughts crowded back like noisy beachcombers.

I went back to the kitchen and asked Karen if she knew of a sound to recite that would stop all the other sounds and then stop itself, so that there would be only the stillness.

She couldn't see the reason for it. "Why do you want to stop things?"

"It's not stopping them, exactly, it's stopping your connection with them." I told her about my idea of pulling the energy out of my electromagnetic systems. "I want the energy to get free, so that I can be still. Do you know what I mean?"

"Mm, maybe." She kept slicing vegetables into her stew, with her back to me, but at least she didn't ask me if I shouldn't be seeing a doctor. Instead she said, "What do you want to be still for?"

I decided to put my cards on the table; the worst she could do was laugh at me. "I don't like always circulating through a lot of thoughts and feelings," I said. "I don't want to be a relative of the fleece-dryer and the Jeep. This is a waste, to be a machine like that."

"Which is a terrible way to look at it," was her view of that. "You're fighting it," she said. "You shouldn't fight things; this is the problem with people: they fight. The whole thing about meditation is to teach you to flow with life."

148

"Why, though? — Listen, can I help with this?" I looked around for another slicing-knife.

"No, just relax, will you?"

"All right." I sat down. "But I don't want to just relax. I don't want this business of flowing with life. Life is ordinarily a mess, and people are ordinarily a mess. I am ordinarily a mess. I can't find myself in all this garbage. I want to be free. I want to get out."

"That's your trouble, okay?" she said, turning her long face around to me for the first time. "If you flowed with life, then you'd already be enjoying yourself, and you wouldn't waste your time wanting to get out."

"What do you recite the sound for, then," I asked her, "if it isn't to stop all this rushing around in your head?"

We had some vigorous arguments. Her idea was to use the sound as a raft: she tried to climb aboard it and then float with the current down the river of ordinary happenings without being upset by them. She knew what I meant by the energy, but she saw it not as a power to help her break free but as a physical sensation to be accepted and enjoyed among the other sensations. She thought I had it backwards to use meditation as a way to resist going along with life. "If you get yourself into this so-called still-ness, what'll you do?" she said. "It'll be death, the ultimate bore."

"The stillness isn't death. What you mean is that it's nothing. It isn't, though. It's something."

"It's something," she mocked. "*What* is it?"

"I don't know. I feel it's right."

"Feel, feel. You're guessing."

"That's right."

"At least you admit it."

My arguments with Karen marked the last boundary of my old life. She confirmed for the first time what I had already come to believe without confirmation: that the energy flowed through other people besides myself. There was no question now that I was imagining things. I was sane. As we argued, a knot of tension

149

at my stomach that I hadn't known was there untied itself and was gone. Karen told me that she'd learnt what she knew about meditation from some friends in Sacramento. I decided to go there and find them when my job at the ranch was finshed. I believed that before long I would know nearly everything that I'd been wanting to learn.

Given our companionship and our isolation, it was inevitable that a physical attraction would strike up between us. Karen felt it before I did: she started smiling as we argued and poking me to make her point. When the meaning of this struck me, a flood of desire dashed across my mind. For months, sexual matters had hardly occurred to me — the disaster in Maine with Margherita had numbed me concerning women. But now there seemed to be no reason to hold back. Why shouldn't I reward myself, I thought, for all the difficulties I've been going through? As far as I was concerned, there was no excuse for any delay.

Even so, I was a bit taken aback by how little delay Karen required. But I was also pleased by it. The way I understood these matters then, you don't take responsibility for a woman's feelings in such a short encounter, and therefore there's no need to pay attention to your own feelings. My job at the ranch was up in a few days, and I presumed that would put an end to the companionship. But as the time approached, I found that I hadn't had my fill, and also that I didn't want to give up the luxury of having someone to talk to. I went into the kitchen and asked Karen how long she intended to cook for these sheepherders for a living.

Her long face was sullen again. "What's it to you," she said.

"My job is up. I want to go West; check out your friends in Sacramento, for example."

"So go."

"I am going, but I'm also enjoying this. I figured maybe you'd come along, look around a bit."

She kneaded her bread vigorously for a while. "I thought you thought your 'systems' are boring."

"What about you? this person who's supposed to flow with life and enjoy herself? I've seen a glacier flow faster. A walrus move faster."

"You've never seen either a glacier or a walrus," was her judgment.

"I have. In travelogues, after the bingo on bingo night." I was performing, the way I used to do in company at home.

"I suppose; why not," she said after a minute, meaning she would go with me.

"You sure you want to disappoint the sheepherders, though?"

"The sheepherders are creeps."

"They're not creeps. It's your mind that creeps. They're just themselves. They think we're creeps. The manager thinks we're all creeps."

"He's not a creep; he's dead."

"You're not flowing with him."

She turned to me. "I don't want to go to Sacramento, Joey. There's somebody there I don't want to see right now."

"So we'll avoid him."

She shook her head. "I'm not going to see those people."

"Where do you want to go, then?"

"We'll pick fruit, okay?" she said.

I didn't want to fight with her about it. I told myself that I could wait to look up these Sacramento people; I could learn more about meditation later. It seemed more important to have Karen come west with me. The truth is that I was very excited by the idea of travelling with a woman. I thought of it as the kind of free and uninhibited life that the people I grew up with would never allow themselves. You'd hear about it occasionally: somebody's neighbor's daughter, and you'd have uncomfortable feelings of envy and of anger that such things were permitted them but not you. Karen seemed as glad and as nervous as I was to leave the ranch; I assumed it was for the same reasons. It didn't occur to me to ask her about it.

We hitchhiked to California, across the Rockies and the Utah flats and the Nevada desert at night, jabbering and poking at each other in a high mood, and exasperating the middle-aged black trucker who drove us and had to listen to us. While we sat beside him in the cab, while the truck barrelled down the high Sierras through the firs and Ponderosa pines, Karen leaned heavily in sleep against me, and I felt a triumph of possession which I had never felt with Margherita, who, unlike Karen, had had so many claims on me. I told myself: after all, you could say that sex is a form of concentration, couldn't you?

We had reached the Sacramento Valley. Karen was awake and looking out. The freeway roared between beans and tomatoes and orchard-trees planted in patches a half-mile square, as if we were touring a vegetable-garden in a planet of giants. The lines of red earth flashed at us between the planted rows. Here and there, earth dikes snaked through flooded fields of green grass: rice, the trucker said. Sometimes near, sometimes far down the flat fields of vegetables, clumps of men in white shirts and straw hats were bent over at the waist, picking. Karen seemed amazed and moved. "*Look* at this," she muttered to herself. "Look at this." Small towns built of neon signs and flaking stucco shot past. In one of them, Karen said suddenly to the trucker: "Stop at the next corner." He stopped. "Come on, Joey," she said.

"What, we getting out?"

"You're so smart."

I thanked the trucker.

"Yeah, sure, buddy," he said. "Happy landings." He sounded like he thought they were very unlikely.

Outside, an overcoat of stifling August air settled on us. In the window of a one-room building with a large crack in its Spanish-style front, a sign said: 'Farm Labor Information.' A thin Mexican with hollow checks drummed his fingers on his desk inside. "Can you pick?" he said. "Any experience?"

152

I was about to tell him what I could do, when Karen said: "Whatever you've got to pick, we can pick."

"Citizens, naturally?" he said.

"Naturally."

He was satisfied. He gave us some papers to fill out and then some directions to a prune-orchard.

"That was pretty smooth of you," I said to Karen afterwards, feeling a bit annoyed; it's uncomfortable to operate according to what you take to be other people's lies. "I haven't ever done this, and neither have you, I guess," I told her.

"He's getting paid, what does he care. We'll need straw hats," was all she said.

The prunes are actually long thin purple plums, drooping thick as rain from scraggly trees. Inching down the orchard rows, the pickers grabbed the fruit and made the trees shake. There were local teenagers who debated baseball at the top of their lungs, and a migrant Mexican crew, men, women, and children, who gossiped tree to tree in a language not too far from my grandparents' Napolitan. I thought I could recognize some of the words. The growers pay by the pound picked, and the Mexicans picked with both hands at an amazing speed. I stood with one foot on my wooden ladder and watched one short plump greying lady place the fruit respectfully into the cloth bag that hung from a belt at her waist; when the bag was full, she eased the plums into a flat wooden box. After I'd tried picking for a few minutes, the plump greying lady, who'd been watching me watch her, said "No-no-no-no-no" and came over to correct me in sign language. I had been sqeezing the fruit as I pulled it down, and my picking-bag had been hanging between my leg and the ladder, ready to be squashed. While the woman was instructing me, I noticed Karen walking back between the trees towards the weighing-in station with a full box of prunes on her right shoulder. She came back without saying anything and began picking again as nimbly and as relentlessly as the Mexicans. "Why didn't you tell me you could do this?" I yelled at her. "You would have saved this lady some trouble."

In reply, Karen cursed me mildly, a habit of hers that never failed to slightly scandalize me. It was one of the things that made me think of her as a drifter, as a woman who wasn't respectable. It was natural of me to think that; as far as I knew, respectable women refused sex without conditions, and besides, I thought nobody respectable, man or woman, would ever think about the mind: that was for outlaws. But as we worked that day and as she corrected my picking, it struck me how little I knew about her: hardly more than her last name. Seeing her with a skill, it came to me for the first time that she must have had a home and that she had a history. She suddenly seemed more formidable and foreign. That night, after we'd bedded down in the orchard near the labor camp, I asked her where she had been.

She said she had grown up on a series of pear-ranches in the small valleys near the Oregon line. Her father was a grower who kept losing his farms. "He lives up there now with my little sister. My older brother is the manager of a big orchard there. My brother is a mental case."

"You mean to want to manage an orchard? Why?"

"I mean he's a mental case. He used to bother me."

"How, bother you?"

"Bother me. Get his hands on me all the time. Keep me from going out with anybody. He beat up one boy I liked and went to jail for it even. There was a whole lot of trouble. Want to know why I'm an expert picker? I have long fingers" — she held them up against the night — "and I picked every summer since I was thirteen. My mother died when I was a junior in high school. So I left."

She had finished her story. I prodded her. "So where'd you go?"

"Oh, Yuba City, Marysville, Sacramento, Fairfield — keep out of that place — one good thing was picking wine-grapes in the

154

Napa Valley." She imitated a connoisseur with an English accent: "Gamay beaujolais. Cabernet sauvignon. I met a nice guy there. He made me finish high school. Then it was time to go to Mexico."

"You went there with this guy?"

"Uh-uh, he went. He had his wife and family back there."

She had finished again. I was getting annoyed at her. "If it's all such a pain in the neck, why not just walk in front of a car, then?"

"You're the one who says life is a mess."

"Is this everything there is, then, the men you've been with?"

She cursed me hotly and said, "I only told you about Hernando"—

"Yeah, sure, Karen, I'm sorry."

She said after a minute: "You're right, though, I did think he was everything there was. I had to be taught he wasn't. I haven't learned what is, though."

"You haven't leaned what is what?"

She said after another minute: "What *is* everything there is, though? What do we want, Joey?"

"I told you. I want to know who I am."

"Why, though?"

"We've been through this. To be a machine is a waste. And don't tell me to flow with it."

"No, okay, okay" — she reached over and pounded my arm. "You can go on wanting to know what you want to know; why should I care what you want? But why do we have to want at all, Joey? That's what I mean: why bother to want all these things we want? All this incredible number of things? You, like with you, it isn't just the place you want to get to in meditation, which you're always talking about, because you certainly want women, for example, and you want to get to sleep when I'm talking too much"—

"I'm listening. I want to hear." I was thinking about the circle of longing that I'd felt reaching out for Margherita, back in Maine in the snow.

"Do you see what I mean?" she said. "I want *something* to be everything there is, and I don't care what it might be, either; just something that would fulfill all the wanting and put an end to it for once. Life is just wanting, wanting, wanting, all the time. If you want a man, you can't just have a man and then finish with wanting him. It always starts again. It's not just men, either: it's the same with everything. Want and want. You're never satisfied. There isn't any peace. It's a trap."

"It's another system," I said.

"It's another system; that's your theory. So what, the theory doesn't help. It doesn't give peace. This is what I want for myself, Joey: peace."

We were silent for a while; I was thinking of home. I said to Karen, "I do think wanting is a system like the others, but it isn't the wanting itself that's the trap. It's believing that your wanting is going to be fulfilled: that's the trap about it. Desire isn't built to be fulfilled, just like you were saying. I have a longing for women — period; I make the longing myself, and Cleopatra couldn't stop it for me. You bleed from the wound whether someone comes along with a bandage or not, so you might as well enjoy the bleeding and forget about healing the thing."

"That's crazy," Karen said. "That's frustration. You don't want frustration. You don't believe that."

"I didn't say frustration. Desire, be fulfilled, desire again. Get hungry, eat, get hungry again. Enjoy it. Flow with it."

She laughed. "Since when did you adopt my side of the argument?"

"Since I started enjoying myself. It's fun to want, and it's fun to have."

She found this extremely amusing. "You immense phony," she called out.

"Be quiet, we're probably not supposed to be sleeping in the

156

orchard."

"Wouldn't it be fun to be kicked out, though? Then all through the night in the smelly cabin you can enjoy your wanting to sleep outside." She crowed with laughter.

I started to protest again, but she interrupted me: "You know something? because this is just what I've been telling myself about you. All this time you've been saying how people should get themselves out of life and into some kind of mystical so-called stillness of so-called energy, but meanwhile you're actually the most maddeningly positive person about life, the most sentimental, nauseatingly happy person I've ever run across, did you know that?" She got up on her elbow with an excited air: "You've never been touched," she said, poking me. "I mean nothing has ever really got to you at the center. You're just bouncing along because you've got that happy little Dago self hidden away inside all smiling about things. You'll never give it up, either. Get out of life, not a chance. It's all just talk."

To defend myself, I told her about Margherita and Vin and about trying to kill myself in the blizzard. After thinking a minute, Karen said: "So what, now your little selfie is all the happier. Proud to have weathered the storm. Yessiree."

Till Karen pointed it out to me, I hadn't realized how much our companionship was changing my thinking. It wasn't that I stopped reciting; during that summer I recited off and on all day as we worked; but my reason for reciting changed. I wanted to summon up the energy not to accumulate it, not to escape all the confusion into the stillness, but to gather it and spend it in feeling and in desire. The weeks seemed to prove me right in what I'd said to her. In the orchards, up on the ladder among the hanging fruits and deep green leaves that hissed in the wind, it seemed a perversion to me to think of desire as desire for something. True desire had no purpose beyond itself. It only made sense in its own purity. Did the trees make the fruit for a purpose, because they wanted something from it? You could say that by their seed they wanted to continue themselves, and that the squirrel, there, enemy of orchardists, made off with the almonds because he wanted to live, but why want to live? What's there to live and continue for, except more life and more continuing and more desire? As I stood still in the orchards, and as the energy poured out of me in my own desire for the fullness of life, I thought that the pure desire for life was itself the fullness of life, the way it is with the embraces of men and women, where urgency is joy, and where completion is exhaustion. Listening to the wind in the leaves, I thought I could feel an energy the same as my own pouring from the pickers as they worked, from the wary squirrels, from the trees, and from Karen, in all their sounds, night and day, the same desire, the same outflowing everywhere, the pure force of living things. This was the essence of beauty. I thought when people once asked that their desire be answered — although what could it be answered with, except with more of itself? — when they stepped out of their desire and began to have, it was then that they stepped out of paradise.

For two months of summer we worked our way northward together up the Sacramento Valley, picking fruit as it ripened — Karen knew just where to go for it: apples, peaches, almonds, plums, more prunes, pears. As we moved north, the great valley narrowed. Beyond the tops of the orchard-trees, the Sierras inched closer, blue in the eastward haze, and the round hills of the Coast Range, lion-colored and studded with sheep and green live-oaks, scattered down nearby on the west. Ahead, in the north, the dark jagged wall of the Trinity Mountains rose slowly higher, as if raised every night by a winch. Watching the mountains, pouring out my energy like a spendthrift to embrace them, I understood that Karen had been right also. Desire was beauty, but it was also tyranny. It took my meditation over. I had slowly less energy to spend. I could think of nothing else but the beauty of the trees, of the warm night air, of my life, and of the womanly form. Sometimes, when for a moment the desire would all have been spent in an embrace, so that I'd see us not as beautiful but as two bodies full of uncomfortable systems in need of cleaning, I'd feel a hot surge of anger against Karen for taking my concentration away from me and disrupting my plans for my life. I didn't tell her this. I knew what had happened was by my own choice. The anger would pass, and I'd ask myself what I'd wanted plans for, anyway? Why do anything but just live?

We talked less. Karen seemed stronger and more content, but she, too, was keeping her thoughts to herself. It was September, still summer in California; we were in Tehama County, at the northern end of the Sacramento Valley. The late prunes had finished early. "We could wait here for the olives, or we could go north for the late pears," Karen said. "Did you ever have a Comice pear? It's the best fruit of all, better than ice-cream. They grow them up there."

She was working up the dirt with a prune-pit as she spoke. Something was up. "Wherever you'd like is okay," I told her.

"I ought to see my little sister," she said.

"So we'll see her."

"You don't mind?"

"Why should I mind?"

In fact, her plan bothered me. I didn't know what she meant by wanting to introduce me to her family. We hadn't spoken about what we would do when the picking-season was over, and I didn't want to speak about it. Arrangements, bargains, plans, commitments, these were all the business of cold weather, the business not of desire but of having.

We hitchhiked north. The highway wound up into the Trinities and then along the bottom of gorges. Tall neat Douglas firs bristled from the steep mountainsides. By three o'clock the highway was in shadow. The stream we camped beside breathed chill on us. The next day at noon, around a bend without warning, Karen's valley widened between the mountains. It was suddenly warmer. On one side of the highway, hay-fields lay still uncut and golden, and on the other side, the orchard-trees, still cluttered with large pears, spread green across the bottomland and lapped at the foot of the mountains like a high wave. Above were more firs that climbed to bare summits. We surprised Karen's father and sister eating lunch in their small cottage in the town. He was grey-haired, long-faced like Karen, with large eyes and loose skin at his neck, a man of fifty who looked sixty-five. The sister was the other strain in the family: a small tightly pretty face made up for high school. They were happy to see Karen and offended that she hadn't warned them she was coming. To me they hardly knew what to say. "We'll be staying at the orchards and picking for Albert," Karen said. Albert was the brother.

"I don't think you should let Albert see Joey with you," said the sister, whose name was Ellen.

"Albert's not making my rules any more," Karen said.

"He doesn't know that, Karrie," Ellen said.

"He's going to know it."

Albert was a short round-faced man in his early thirties. He managed the pear-orchard for the owners. He had light balding hair, thick arms, and triangular eyes. He looked Karen up and down with amusement and contempt and it seemed to me with a trace of lust. "Well, what do you know," he said when he saw her.

"Nothing I'd tell you," she said.

"If you're not going to act polite, old girl, I'm not going to sign you up. We're full already. They all want to work this year."

"Sign us up," she said.

He looked at me for the first time, his eyes resting on me dully. Then he went behind his desk. "Your name?"

I told Karen afterwards: "Maybe we should stay in town, like your sister said."

"Did Albert bother you or something?" She was brightly excited and nervous: the same mood I'd seen in her when we were getting ready to leave the sheep-ranch in Wyoming.

"I don't want to be around a guy like that," I said. "I don't like the way he looked at you or at me either."

"He'll be all right," she said.

"That's what you say," I told her, "but your sister said I shouldn't let him see me with you, and your sister's been here, while you haven't, and she's going to know how"—

Karen interrupted me: "Albert's got my sister and everybody else so uptight they're afraid to hardly even look at him. It's too expensive to stay in town, Joey. The labor-camp is okay here."

I argued for a while, but her mind was fixed on it. We settled our gear in one of a group of cabins beside an outside cooking-area at the edge of the orchard.

Pickers were already busy among the trees. The Comice pears are thinned back to eight or ten to the lateral branch, so that the mature fruits weigh well over a half a pound apiece, worth as much as a dollar a fruit in the gift-pack trade. The pickers had to treat the pears with reverence, since the slightest bruise took them off the premium market. Albert spent most of his time tearing through the orchards in his white Jeep pickup-truck, stopping suddenly, hurling himself out, and shouting at one Mexican picker after another to slow down and take care. He cursed them, and they heard him with quiet hatred. A dozen times a day he would stop by the tree Karen and I would be picking, and he'd curse her the same way, impersonally as another picker, or else he would tease her without humor, with the half-intimate remarks that a teenaged boy might make to his sister who's in the process of maturing. Karen returned Albert's insults almost gaily. Me he ignored. This went on for several days. I told Karen that she only excited her brother by talking back to him. "You should treat him like you treated the sheepherders," I said. "Give him nothing."

"I've done that, Joey. That's all I ever gave him. I'm not going to do it any more."

"Is that what you came back home for, to have it out with him?"

"I thought he wouldn't talk to me. I just wanted Dad and Ellen to stop worrying about me, isn't that all right?"

"Yeah, you could have told me I was going to be Exhibit A. I could have prepared my nerves for it."

We were talking on the ladders, and I remember she started eating a pear that had ripened — something the pickers are forbidden. "This has nothing to do with you," she said.

"Nothing except I'm the football in this football-game you're having with Albert. The whole thing's unhealthy. You're the one who told me he's a mental case. What makes you think it's any good to have a contest with a mental case?"

"I'm going to win," she said calmly, eating her pear. "These are just incredibly good, Joey."

I was furious at her. "If all this has nothing to do with me, then I'm getting out."

"Hey, don't, okay? Joey?" She reached over to me through the branches. "I don't want to always be running away from him." Her hand fell on my wrist. "Just a few more days?"

I let her have her way. She had never asked anything of me before. But their war had unnerved me. That night, I stood on the ladder among the leaves in the cool air and tried to feel the delight that I had felt all summer; and looking at her as she slept, I tried to remember the desire I had had for her, but it was all clouded. All I felt was anger and uncertainty. I tried to recite a sound, but I couldn't concentrate my mind. I blamed her. I cursed myself for following her to that valley. She should have gone on there alone, and I could have met her again afterwards, or maybe not — maybe we had had enough of each other. I ought to be looking for people to teach me about meditation, I ought to be looking for the stillness, instead of loafing like this and spending my energy and growing a lot of entanglements. I decided to tell her at the end of the week that I was going to Sacramento to look up her friends there and that she could come with me or not, just as she liked — although, once I'd decided this, I realized that I still wanted her to come with me.

Albert was beginning to understand that he had lost control of her. He began looking at me when he came up to us in the orchard. He would stare at me as if he was trying to decide how to account for me and what to do about me. I tried joking with him. Without answering, he would turn away slowly and say something to Karen. It must have been obvious to him that I was afraid of him. I gave up even making an attempt to recite; it seemed to me his voice was always in the orchard. Two days passed; I was planning to tell Karen that night about my decision to go on to Sacramento. But events came too fast for my plans. That afternoon, just before quitting time, before I'd gotten around to talking to Karen, Albert tried to run me down with his pickup-truck. I had been walking to the collection-shed with a lug of pears on my shoulder. There was traffic on the highway nearby, and I hadn't heard Albert coming. At the last moment I caught sight of the truck out of the corner of my eye. I hurled myself aside from the track. The fender of the truck caught me on the hip with a hollow thump and knocked me down. Immediately Albert was out of the truck and standing over me as I began to get up. His hands were opening and closing. Mexicans were watching us from among the trees. I stood up; it seemed my hip was only bruised. The pears I'd been carrying had scattered over the ground. "You bruised them," Albert said, kicking them. He looked at the pickers watching him; the orchard was silent. Seeming to decide, he got back into his truck, stared at me a moment, and drove off.

I limped back to our cabin, feeling shaken and nauseated. My legs and arms were unstable. I began packing up my gear. In a few minutes, Karen's steps were outside. "Joey? Joey?" She ran into the cabin. "Joey, are you all right? Roberto told me" — Roberto was the crew-boss. "Listen, are you all right? Let me see" —

I didn't want to talk to her; I only wanted to get out of that place. I kept on rolling up my sleeping-bag as she stood over me, saying, "Joey, where'd you get hit? I'm sorry, I'm really sorry" —

Her distress irritated me. The fright I'd felt flew out in anger. "What are you sorry for?" I said loudly, without looking at her. "You're winning your contest with him, aren't you?"

"It wasn't, though — I didn't mean" — Her voice trailed off. She began packing up her stove and the eating-gear. She was putting it together sloppily and crying. This infuriated me. I wanted to hurt her. "Why don't you stay behind for the last round and wrap it up?" I said.

We packed in silence. I had a head start on her, and she had more things. As I was lashing my sleeping-bag to my back-pack, she came over to me and laid her hand on my arm. "Joey, listen"—

"Listen what."

"Don't? Don't do this, just go like this?"

"You want me to wait around for his next move?"

"No — no I don't, but"—

I set the back-pack upright against the bed. When I squatted down to hoist it, my bruised hip gave, and I stumbled forward onto my hands. As I righted myself, Karen squatted down next to me. "We could meet in Yreka tomorrow?" she said. "At the bus-station, and talk about it"—

I was trying to rise with the back-pack; she was holding me by the arm with both hands. "Just talk about it?" she said.

I shouted at her, "Cut it out, will you?" and I threw up my arm that she was holding, so that her arms flew back against her face. I heard the crystal of her wristwatch crunch against her cheekbone, and she stumbled backward and cried out. She stood bent over, holding her face in her hands. I was furious at her for having made me hurt her. I said: "Why should I want to travel with you any more?" She waited a minute, seeming to hiccough, and then without taking her hands away from her face she turned around and ran out the door.

For a moment I felt numbed; then I called out, "Karen? Hey, Karen?" I limped to the door and looked after her; she didn't look back. I stood for a while leaning in the doorway, hardly thinking, watching the point where she had disappeared among the trees. The wave of anger had passed. I felt spent. Nearby, in the bare space between the cabins and the orchard, women were lighting fires in the cooking-pits. I watched them dully. Beyond them and beyond the trees, the sun was setting among streaks of clouds that were divided by the western mountains. Roberto, the crew-boss, a small man with a lined face who chain-smoked by inhaling fiercely through his nostrils, stood talking among a group of men who were seated on benches near the women. I roused myself and went over to them and asked Roberto whether anyone had seen Karen. There was a discussion in Spanish. "Louis saw her running towards the office a couple minutes ago," Roberto said. He meant Albert's office; there was a first-aid cabinet there and a pay-phone. Louis, a plump man who had eight children, seven of them boys, added something in Spanish. The men all looked at me curiously.

Favoring my hip, and keeping to the trees to avoid Albert in case he might come down the track in his Jeep, I walked slowly towards the office. The orchard was deserted and silent now but for the evening voices of birds. I felt tremendously discouraged. I wanted to repair things with Karen, but repairing things and travelling with her again would only make it inevitable that we would wreck things again and do each other more harm. It seemed to me that every friendship I had ever made, with Margherita, Vin, my stunt-pals, the monsignor, Lonny, and with Karen, had all ended in damage and confusion. Anger had flown into everything like a cloud of flies. There would be no finding a woman as long as I desired her; I would always be lost in the deafening cloud of my own feelings. The other people were invisible.

Ahead through the trees, I could see Albert's truck parked beside the office. I stopped walking and wavered a moment, trying to convince myself that his anger was probably spent also, and that he would ignore me if I went in there looking for Karen. But I was too afraid of him even to step out onto the driveway, in case he might catch sight of me through the office-window, though at that hour he was very likely not in the office at all, but in his living-quarters behind. And what if I did go in and he did attack me? What was I planning to do that was so precious? If I found people in Sacramento to help me out, I would probably manage to mess up their lives somehow in return and end up back where I started anyway, so what was I protecting? My fear of Albert infuriated me and humiliated me to myself, but it held me. After a minute, I turned around to go back to the cabin, to wait for Karen there.

The orchard was in twilight. Squirrels were chattering in the shadows. I remembered thinking of the squirrels two months before; I had thought their simple desire to survive without asking why was something perfect, a recollection of paradise. The thought was laughable to me now. It seemed to me a mockery, not bliss but bitterness, not to know the reason for all this work of living. It was a humiliation to be driven by the desire for life and by the fear of losing it, when for all I knew it was worth nothing. What could it be worth, if there was only desire and never any having that would last for longer than an instant? The pickers with their children, Albert with his fighting, the orchard-owners with their money, Karen with her dreamed-of ease, and I with my search for myself: we all believed there would be a time of having, a time that unlike all the other times would stay and be held, instead of bursting like a bubble in our hands. There were no times. We would keep nothing. Only the desire continued, grasping but never holding, a hand grasping at itself, grasping at air.

The sound of Albert's truck was in the orchard. I stood still: it was moving down the driveway towards the cabins. In a minute, the truck-door slammed, and through the quiet evening I heard Albert shouting in a tone of fury: "Roberto? Where's Roberto?" There was a low-voiced answer. I limped hurriedly through the trees. Albert was cursing foully, and I could hear Roberto's voice protesting in answer, though I couldn't make out the words. After a few minutes, I reached the edge of the trees. Albert and Roberto, now silent, stood facing each other by the cooking-fires. In a semi-circle, a group of men-pickers watched; the women had disappeared. By its gleam in the firelight, I caught sight of a knife in Albert's hand. Suddenly he and Roberto circled around one another so that Albert's back was to me. I walked quickly out across the bare space and joined the watching pickers. Beside me stood a teenaged boy who spoke English. "Why are they fighting, hey?" I asked him.

"He says Roberto hit his sister," the boy said.

The two men were circling again; someone had handed Roberto a knife as well. It dawned on me that back at the office, Albert must have challenged Karen as to who had struck her, and that she must have lied and blamed it on Roberto, in order to give me a chance get away. But the pickers had been nearby our cabin when I'd hit her, and right afterwards I'd asked them if they'd seen her; they must have known the truth. I said to the boy next to me: "Hasn't Roberto told Albert it was me?'

The boy looked at me curiously and with mild hostility, but without anger. Instead of answering, he nodded to the fighters. The two men were watching each other intently, their eyes shifting, their mouths tight with the grievances of years. The thought jumped through my mind that Karen knew what she was doing when she lied and blamed it on Roberto: I ought to slip away; these two have probably fought before, maybe often. Roberto can defend himself; they probably enjoy fighting; I should slip away. The thoughts tempted me. It was a relief to think I'd be able to escape from this crazy valley. We could repair things together; we could begin again. But even as I thought these things, I couldn't get myself to move from where I stood. The idea of risking Roberto's life so that I could get away was too harsh for me to stomach. I couldn't let myself be responsible for it; it would be more than I wanted to live with. The future was already too discouraging. For

167

all I knew, Roberto was also discouraged with his life, but he still must believe that time held something for him, although it surely held nothing for him but more belief and more discouragement. But there was no sense in his taking my place, when I no longer believed.

Albert suddenly lunged out at him, and Robert jumped back; the crowd of men shouted. I looked around: there were some ladders propped up against one of the cabins. Walking quickly around behind the watching men, I took down one of the ladders, and holding it straight out in front of me like a battering-ram, I pushed my way throught the crowd, then stepped up to the fighters, and swung the ladder up and down and back and forth between them to separate them. Both of them jumped back and shouted at me angrily. Albert grabbed at the ladder, but I swung it up quickly, rapping his arm. He cursed me and ordered me to get out of there. I answered: "I hit Karen. Roberto didn't. You're fighting him for nothing."

"Keep out of the way, will you? This is my business," he said furiously in a low voice. I think he was embarrassed to have his mistake proved in front of the Mexicans. He was breathing heavily; the sweat on his face shone in the firelight. The pickers were silent.

"Karen lied to you, so as to protect me from you," I said. "It was me that hit her. Fighting Roberto is a waste."

Someone muttered in Spanish: "Vamos, Roberto."

Albert looked from Roberto to me, confusion clouding his triangular eyes.

"Why do you fight at all?" I said.

There were footsteps behind me. A knife landed by my heels. Roberto and the others vanished in the deepening evening. Albert looked at me, his eyes moving around me. "She wanted to protect you," he said quietly.

"Yes."

"She wanted to protect you." He seemed to be rearranging his anger in his mind. He moved towards me, then reached out suddenly to grab the ladder. I backed up, jerking the ladder away from him. He lunged at the ladder twice more as I backed away. Then he reached out with his foot and kicked aside the knife that one of the pickers had thrown me. He nodded to himself. It struck me that he had planned how to get the knife out of my reach. He hadn't actually been trying to grab my ladder yet. It amazed me that he would take the trouble to have plans in his fights, the way other people might plan a day's work or an outing in the country. But why wouldn't he plan? He suddenly seemed to me no different than everyone else. He wanted things, and when he got what he wanted, what then? He didn't know. Desire burned in him, more hotly than in other people, maybe, but with the same fire, and afterwards he would be left with the same ashes.

Someone had started up Albert's truck. It was Karen. She was calling to me to circle around him and escape. Albert tensed and watched me intently. The desire to get away from him flashed through me again: I felt it attack my body like a shooting flame. I didn't want to obey my desires any longer. I dropped the ladder in front of me and sat down on the ground.

From Albert came a noise of surprise; then he said harshly: "You get up." Hot fear roared inside me; Albert himself seemed distant compared to it. But what good could there be in escaping him, if fire still lived inside me and ruled me? Wasn't this why Karen had come home and faced him: to put out her own fear? I told myself that my vow to take control of my feelings and make my mind my own, this vow I'd given up almost everything else but my life for, would be nothing but a joke if I ignored it now when the test came. I wasn't going to ignore it. I wasn't going to let all my work and my hopes become a joke. I called up all my stubbornness, and looking past where Albert stood over me, I tried to concentrate my mind on the dying campfire.

The shadows of the flames flickered across the ground, over the truck, across the trees behind. Not listening to Albert's voice, I

169

tried to follow with my eyes as each flame threw its shadow like a leaping body across the dark leaves. Above the orchard, between the mountain peaks, the sky was alight with the last orange of evening. Albert was moving; he kicked me hard in the right thigh. After a moment, he spoke again and tossed a knife at my feet. Reflections of the firelight trembled on the blade. The hot pain in my thigh seemed to flow out into the air and down into the ground, to join the fire of the burning world.

In my mind I gave Albert my life if he wanted it. I felt the giving as a release, as a gladness. Gates in my chest locked by tension seemed to fly open and to let some nameless animal go. Suddenly Albert kicked me again, but more lightly, as if he wanted to rouse me. I heard his voice call out clearly, in a mild and puzzled tone:

"Hey, Karen, what do you see in this guy? He's strange."

She called: "Are you all right now, Albert?"

"I didn't cut him, Karrie."

"That was right, Albert. You want to come over to Dad and Ellen's with me now?"

"Sure, okay, Karrie."

He spoke meekly, like a boy to his parents after he's done something wrong. His steps trudged across the driveway. The truck-door slammed. As I listened, as they drove off together, my body seemed to open slowly at every point in my skin, then at every point inside me. The energy welled up from within. Like cool water it flowed out in a moving stillness, across the open borders of my skin, across the ground, around the farmworkers regathering near me, around and through them, through the trees, as if they all were shadows of the dying fire. They seemed to tremble and dissolve. I looked for myself. I too had dissolved into the energy. Without the desire burning inside me, what could hold me in? Celebrisi had gone; I didn't have to look for him any longer. There was only the energy flowing in stillness. I thought this in a burst of happiness, and then the river of my thoughts, silent at last, spread out onto a shining sea.

EPILOGUE

I NOTICED IT was day. Leaves and wind were around my head. I saw I was standing on a ladder in a tree still bent with fruit, with my arms embracing the trunk and my head turned aside on my arms. When had I climbed there? Had I slept? For a moment there seemed to be no past. Then I felt the sensation again in my body of walking through the orchard in the last hour of the evening before, of having no weight, of my mind growing and filling the valley till the mountains were resting just beside me and the stars stood close by in the night. I'd recited, and the dark cliffs had rung with the syllable silently.

The peace of having surrendered my desire returned to me now in the morning. I seemed to enter the very center of the syllable, and my thoughts quieted and ceased. Time disappeared. The surf of the energy was rolling back into my mind, was crashing in stillness in from the trees, the mountains, the waking cabins nearby, and the high clouds. I was within them, and they were all within me. Their sounds were complete within my mind. As the farmworkers, slow with sleep, stepped out of the cabin doors, the force that gave each his own or her own life, hidden at the center of each of them, flowed within my own heart. What could make any one of us separate from any other, if the shields of desire and thought and time were set down in peace and joy? How could even one be marked apart, any more than the light of lamps could be divided when their shades were lifted away?

Words had begun in my mind; time was passing again. Watching the women light the cooking-fires reminded me of Karen and Albert. I began climbing down the ladder with the idea of relieving myself and getting something to eat, and suddenly it occurred to me that there would be a future.

I ate breakfast in a roadside café near the orchard gate, feeling delighted with the food, and strange. What was I to do in this future I had, now that for a second time I had given up my life, only to find it returned to me? In the winter, in Quebec, it hadn't mattered what I did — to choose among all the equally meaning-less futures could be nothing but guesswork, because all my knowledge had been taken from me. Now, again, I couldn't find in my thoughts any reason to do one thing over another; I seemed once more to know nothing. It was true that anything was the same as anything else this time not because there there was no meaning, but because everything shared a single meaning of energy and delight. But that was no help in choosing. I did want to clear things up with Karen, go apologize, wipe up that dark spot on the past. I didn't want to keep on with her, at least not there in her valley; and her job was to stay in the valley and finish the work of her independence. But besides that? What job in what place, what landscape and new people? Would I always end up moving from stopping-place to stopping-place and state to state, or would I find a home at last among friends who had travelled before me? Was there a chance ever to answer the wish that came in the early mornings, to see my son again? If I could speak to him, what would I tell him, what place could I point to and ex-plain: this is myself? Who was Celebrisi? That was what I had asked myself almost a year before in Quebec, and I still couldn't even begin to say.

Thinking these things, I could feel the muscles tighten in my body: in my right leg, my left arm, across my shoulders, my face, my backside. The energy receded. I walked back to the cabin to pick up my gear, feeling closed into my ordinary mind, and the living presence of the orchard was hidden again in the leaves and the wood. I knew what it was: I knew what those muscles were trying to hold in: a private, separate self, a Celebrisi of the future and the past.

Suddenly I remembered asking myself who I was at other times, but with a different meaning. It was during the stunts, back at home. I'd pretend to be someone I never was, and at the height of concentration I'd ask myself 'Who's Celebrisi?' to strengthen the feeling that for a moment I didn't know. 'Who's Celebrisi?' Walking down the highway in Karen's valley, I asked it again with that same delight, with a joyous knowledge that I would never know. There could be no answer, except by my holding on to a separate self that shut out my true nature. Why hold onto it, then? Give it away! What did I need of the past, what was the past made of but anger and grievance for what went wrong, and longing for what once went well? What did I care for the future, since it had no power to exist except in my own fear and nervousness and desire? What else was this self but the hand of thought grasping at time? Who's Celebrisi? Let there be no Celebrisi, let there be no self, let there be no past, no future, let there be only presence, and the pure energy of life. If I desire anything, let me recite it away. If I gain anything, let me give it away; if I lose something, let me be glad, and if any thoughts of self or past or future arise in my mind, let me ask who? Who thinks this? Then I will remember that there is always only the present. Then the orchards, the valley, the mountains, the cities, and the other people will ring with the silent celebration of being.

ABOUT THE PUBLISHER

The Buddhist Text Translation Society was formed in 1972 with the goal of making the genuine teachings of Buddhism available to the Western reader. All the Society's translators are not only scholars but practicing Buddhists, and each translation is accompanied by an explanatory commentary directed to a modern audience. Since 1972, BTTS has published some twenty works: translations of major Buddhist writings, handbooks of instruction in meditation, and books growing out of the expanding Buddhist experience in America.

In preparation are translations, with commentary, of the three crowning texts of the Buddhist Mahayana: the *Shurangama Sutra,* the *Lotus Sutra,* and the *Avatamsaka Sutra*. The work of the Buddhist Text Translation Society is carried out under the direction of the Venerable Ch'an Master Hsuan Hua, Abbot of Gold Mountain Monastery in San Francisco.

A list of BTTS publications appears on the following pages.

From The Buddhist Text Translation Society

The Amitabha Sutra, with commentary by the Venerable Ch'an Master Hua. 184 pages, $5.95.

"All through the history of Chinese Buddhism, Ch'an (Zen) Masters have spoken highly of the Pure Land doctrines, and have recommended recitation of the name of Amitabha Buddha as the surest and simplest path to enlightenment. The Pure Land Sutras teach that the Buddha, seeing that, in the degenerate age which is now upon us, it would be increasingly difficuty for ordinary beings to practice the profound teachings set forth in the earlier sutras, spontaneously revealed an easier path well within the capability of all. . .

"Master Hua's book on *The Amitabha Sutra* opens with a number of sections of an introductory nature, and then proceeds to discourse upon the text of the Sutra sentence by sentence. . . The language is refreshingly modern and down-to-earth, and the substance is pleasantly varied with poems, amusing anecdotes, and sage aphorisms. . . Master Hua's text, though intensely serious in purpose, is full of gaiety."
— John Blofeld, author of *The Wheel of Life,* in *Shambhala Review of Books and Ideas,* formerly *Codex Shambhala,* September, 1975.

The Vajra Sutra, with commentary by the Venerable Master Hua. The central concepts of emptiness, non-attachment, and non-dwelling. The Sutra that enlightened the Sixth Patriarch. 192 pages, $5.95.

The Great Compassion Dharani Sutra, with commentary by the Venerable Master Hua. From the Secret School of Buddhism, the Sutra on the uses and power of the Great Compassion Mantra. With 84 pages of rare Secret School woodcuts. The first translation into any Western language. 352 pages, $10.

Sutra of the Past Vows of Earth Store Bodhisattva. The classic Buddhist description of the workings of karma. With commentary by the Venerable Master Hua. A work widely known in China, now in English for the first time. 235 pages, $6.75 paper, $12.75 cloth.

The Sutra in Forty-Two Sections. The Buddha's instructions in the essentials of the path. The first Buddhist Sutra to be introduced into China. With the Master's commentary. 100 pages, $3.25.

Pure Land and Ch'an Dharma Talks. Practical instruction in the methods of recitation and meditation. By the Venerable Master Hua. 72 pages, $3.00.

The Ten Dharmarealms Are Not Beyond a Single Thought. An illustrated handbook of the realms of being as Buddhism describes them. Poems and commentary by the Venerable Master Hua. Second edition. 72 pages, $3.00.

Buddha Root Farm. Instruction in meditation on the name of Amitabha Buddha. Buddhists consider recitation of the Buddha's name to be the surest, easiest path to enlightenment. By the Venerable Master Hua. 72 pages, $3.00.

Records of the Life of the Venerable Master Hua, Vol. I. The remarkable story of the early life of a sage, and a vivid glimpse of the religious life of China under the Republic. 96 pages, $3.95.

Records of the Life of the Venerable Master Hua, Vol. II. The Master's years in Hong Kong in the 1950's. 230 pages, $6.95.

The Sixth Patriarch's Dharma Jewel Platform Sutra. The founding text of Ch'an Buddhism. The life and teachings of the Venerable Master Hui Neng, the Sixth Patriarch.

All BTTS books are paperbound, except where noted otherwise. They may be obtained at bookstores or by mail directly from the publisher at 1731 Fifteenth Street, San Francisco, California 94103. (California residents add 6-1/2% sales tax.)

Bookstores may obtain BTTS books from the publisher or from Book People, distributors, 2940 Seventh Street, Berkeley, California 94710.